I0590734

EPIC IS HER FUTURE

SCHOOL OF NECESSARY MAGIC™ BOOK EIGHT

JUDITH BERENS   MARTHA CARR   MICHAEL ANDERLE

DISRUPTIVE IMAGINATION

EPIC IS HER FUTURE TEAM

Thanks to Early Readers

Debi Sateren
Michael Robbins
Kathleen Fettig
Terry Hicks Bennett
Bep Hvilsted-Koopman

Thanks to the JIT Readers

Misty Roa
Nicole Emens
John Ashmore
Daniel Weigert
Mary Morris
Peter Manis
Danika Fedeli
Thomas Ogden
Keith Verret
Angel LaVey
Paul Westman

If we've missed anyone, please let us know!

DEDICATIONS

From Martha

To everyone who still believes in magic
and all the possibilities that holds.
To all the readers who make this
entire ride so much fun.
And to my son, Louie and so many wonderful friends who
remind me all the time of what
really matters and how wonderful
life can be in any given moment.

From Michael

To Family, Friends and
Those Who Love
To Read.
May We All Enjoy Grace
To Live The Life We Are
Called.

CHAPTER ONE

Alison waited patiently for the more eager commuters to leave the train before she lifted her suitcase and stepped onto the platform. Her friends stood in a tightknit group near a pillar, chatting enthusiastically. She smiled as the familiar excitement pushed the nerves and apprehension aside. This was their last New Year's at the school.

She was excited to begin her final semester, but the question of moving immediately on to college remained in the back of her mind. A gap year had seemed like a good idea, but Brownstone and Shay had made it clear how they felt about it, and she was coming around to their way of thinking. Keep on track for her goals, and stay with her age group, her father had said. Still, the idea was there, percolating. She liked the idea of traveling for a year, maybe getting the chance to see Izzie.

Kathleen spotted her first. The redhead squealed with excitement and waved enthusiastically, new bracelets jangling on her slender wrist. She abandoned her luggage and rushed to pull her friend into a tight hug. Alison hugged her back, grateful to be pulled out of the thoughts swirling in her head.

"This is it. Our last New Year's here. Aren't you excited?"

"Of course. Did you have a good Christmas?"

Kathleen looped her arm around Alison's and guided her back to the group.

"It was absolutely wonderful. My parents got me these stunning fairy-made bracelets. They're incredibly rare."

Alison raised an eyebrow and glanced at the sparkling jewelry.

"Are you sure it's a good idea to bring them to school?"

"Oh, yes, they're enchanted so they can't be stolen. It was an expensive security measure but worth it. Don't you think?"

Alison pushed her glasses up her nose and admired the pretty stones. In her Drow sight, they glowed with the faint blue of peaceful magic. With her glasses, they were a string of delicate white stones with tiny silver chain links. It must have taken a very steady hand to create such fine workmanship.

Tanner came close and kissed Alison's cheek.

"I was worried when the train was delayed. Mrs. Beasley is meeting us, and you know how she hates to wait."

"We should get moving." Ethan picked up his new bag. "I don't know about you, but I don't fancy walking all the way back to the school."

"Oh, she wouldn't." Kathleen pushed her hair from her

eyes and straightened her pale-pink scarf. "She's all growl and no bite."

They made their way between the last straggling commuters and up the complicated stairways.

"What did everyone get for Christmas?" Kathleen asked the group. "Anything exciting?"

"Shay adopted me officially as her daughter," Alison said casually.

"Oh, my God, that's amazing." Emma grinned. "You must be so happy! This means you're finally free of your father, right?"

Tanner held Alison a little closer, offering support against the dark memories.

"Yes. I have a complete family." The memory of her Drow mother flashed in her mind.

Emma frowned at the flatness of her friend's tone. She should have been grinning and joyous.

"I'm sorry, I shouldn't have brought up that awful memory." She squeezed Alison's arm. "Are you okay?"

"Of course she is. She'll be a badass bounty hunter like Brownstone. Nothing can keep her down for long," Peter declared.

"I got a beautiful elf-made dress." Kathleen paused for their full attention. "And a private workshop with the fashionista Madam Tae."

Emma and Aya stopped in their tracks, their mouths open. They'd listened to Kathleen talk about fashion enough to understand the enormity of her statement. The others were lost.

"Madam Tae? As in the elusive elf who runs the hottest

fashion line?" Emma put her hand on Kathleen's arm. "How did you pull that off?"

Kathleen's smiled and drew herself taller, leading the group around the first bend in the stairs.

"It's a case of who you know, not what you know."

"Congratulations!" Alison's smile broadened. She understood how much this meant to her friend. "Will this be in the summer before college?"

"Yes. I can't wait. I'm putting together a list of questions. I hope she'll help me get into my dream college, Parsons School of Design. My grades are good, and I obviously have the flair they need. I'm the perfect person to bring magic into the fashion world and show everyone what can be achieved… I hope."

Emma smiled encouragement. "I'm sure you'll be accepted. You've put too much work in for them to reject you."

"I got clothes for Christmas. My parents didn't want to encourage the melding of technology and magic." Peter frowned. "They haven't forgiven me for the minion experiment."

Alison and Tanner looked at each other.

"Do we want to know?" Tanner asked.

"It sounds so much worse than it really was. I combined pixie magic with small toy robots to form minions to help around the kitchen. Once I had perfected those, I could begin looking into something more akin to golems." Peter almost bumped into a particularly aggressive wizard who tried to run down the wrong side of the stairs. "Unfortunately, the pixie magic reacted poorly to confinement in the small space of the metal robot."

Alison tried to hold back a smile when she saw where this was going.

"The robot did a fine job helping me bake cookies. It trotted across the counter to bring me a cup of flour when...well, it exploded."

Kathleen fixed him with a disappointed look. "Does everything you make explode?" Perhaps you need to focus on more practical things. Unless you plan to move into military magic."

He sighed. "It was one small mistake. I'm making good progress on the new version. I used my own pure magic this time as it's easier to bind and control."

"Please don't blow up our room." Ethan's grin was good-natured. "I'd rather not sleep in the woods."

They were almost at the top of the final set of stairs when a pair of gnomes barreled up behind them. The newcomers paused, stared at the sign for Charlottesville, and cursed in three separate languages before running down again.

Emma pursed her lips. "They really should put better signs up here. It's so easy to get lost."

"Running up and down these is a good way to get fit, though." Tanner gestured at the stairs.

Kathleen wrinkled her nose. "I don't see why they can't add elevators."

"Would you like servants to carry your bags, too?" Aya teased.

Kathleen thought for a long moment, and the group laughed.

They split into pairs to avoid drawing too much attention as they passed through the wall into the Starbucks.

5

Alison hung back with Tanner and enjoyed the peace when they had the stairway to themselves. The knowledge that this was both a beginning and an end stirred butterflies in her stomach. He stroked her hair and smiled gently with understanding.

Thankfully, the Starbucks was mostly empty when they wound between the chairs and tables. The staff was used to the odd comings and goings and ignored them entirely. Cheerful Christmas music played from the speakers. They stepped out into the bright clear sunshine and saw Luke standing with Mrs. Beasley and her jitney, waiting for them.

To his dismay, a particularly excitable pair of dachshunds bounded up to him, dragging their bedraggled owner after them. The small dogs circled the shifter's legs, wagging their tails eagerly as though they'd found their long-lost best friend.

"Oh, I'm sorry. I don't know what's gotten into them."

Luke helped the woman disentangle the leashes from his limbs while the dogs jumped and tried to lick his face. Being a shifter had some downsides, and he was relieved they were short-legged and unable to try to sniff his butt. Thank goodness for small blessings.

Jason Parker watched, unnoticed as the friends ascended the stairs. A knot formed in his stomach as he held back, allowing them to move well ahead. So much had changed since that fateful day almost a year ago. He had been full of fire and conviction that his actions were right.

From a distance, Professor Eleanor Hudson kept an eye on him, still questioning whether it was a good idea to have given him a second chance. Still, the headmistress, Mara Berens had argued in favor of it. The goal was never to wipe out the dark families, she had said. Enough with the destruction, and if that wasn't the goal, then reconciliation was going to be necessary.

Eleanor winced remembering how Xander Powell had slammed the door on his way out of the meeting. Jason Parker was going to be allowed to come back. Mara Berens was determined to build a better world and Jason wanted to change. It was an opportunity, not a mistake.

"So be it," she whispered, drawing the hooded cloak closer around her face, and whispering the spell that changed her appearance just enough to hide her identity. "But, I'm not as sure as you are old friend that a dark wizard can change that much. We shall see."

Something dark caught Jason's eye as he climbed the wooden stairs, brushing past all the commuters. Frowning, he peered into the corner of the platform to identify a shape or movement. Seeing a faint flicker, a shiver passed through him. A sudden sensation of being watched flared and his instincts told him to run—far and fast and never look back. Instead, he swallowed hard and kept moving, heading for the Starbucks and his return to the school.

"It's a new day, it's got to be." He said it with as much conviction as he could muster, even as his stomach soured.

"Watch where you're going!" An older elf, late for work snapped at Jason, brushing past him on the way to the top. Jason startled, gripping the wand in his pocket, even as he put his head down, continuing to climb toward his new life, back where it had all gone so wrong.

Mrs. Beasley wore a bright blue coat and a thick, yellow scarf wrapped tightly with the tassels hanging almost to her knees. Her matching yellow bobble hat was pulled low, giving her a comical appearance.

"Come on. You're not the only ones who want to see New Year's." She grinned and held out a white paper bag. "Have a butterscotch candy."

Luke grinned at his friends. Peter pulled him into a hug while his silver luggage made its own way to the luggage hold.

"How've you been?"

Luke shrugged a shoulder and smiled. "Not bad. Glad to be back here, though. Good Christmas?"

"I got a long lecture about how my experiments are dangerous." Peter rolled his eyes.

Luke laughed and turned to the others. "Great to see you. How was your Christmas?"

Two wizards brushed past him and boarded the jitney, glancing back with a look at him.

"I see some things haven't changed," he muttered.

Tanner made a point of hugging his friend. "Good to see you. We'll have an awesome year. I can feel it."

The shifter tried to brush off the snub. He focused instead on greeting everyone else.

The students stowed their bags, and each took a candy. Peter popped his into his mouth, but Alison inspected hers, checking for magic. Seeing none, she slipped it between her lips and smiled at the rich, creamy taste.

"I only deal in the very best candy." Mrs. Beasley winked.

The group claimed the rear of the bus, leaving the front seats for the scattering of juniors who had returned to the school a few days early. There were always students who would rather wander the quiet halls than remain at home. A flush of happiness filled Alison as she thought back to her own home and family. With her only home for the holidays and summers, Brownstone was still adjusting to having a daughter. He sometimes seemed a little bewildered as to how to deal with a teenage girl, but his heart was always in the right place. Shay had beamed with pride on seeing Alison's grades and hearing her plans to study criminal psychology at college.

Peter put his hand in his pocket, and his face pinched.

"Don't you dare bring any of your gadgets or experiments to life on my bus." Mrs. Beasley glared at him from her seat.

He held his hands up.

"I wouldn't dare, Mrs. Beasley. When have I ever damaged your bus?" He smiled sweetly.

She narrowed her eyes but let it slide. Admittedly, he'd never damaged the bus, but he had caused havoc.

"Have you heard from Izzie?" Peter leaned over the seat.

Alison braced herself as the bus moved off, shaking her head. "Nothing, and I expected some contact over Christmas."

Luke stared out the window, his shoulders tight. He

missed her and had hoped she'd leave Alison a note to give to him.

"Maybe the headmistress will have something." Tanner squeezed Alison's hand. "She's family."

Alison nodded. He was right. Maybe it was safer to send something to the school instead.

A thin layer of snow coated the ground as they made their way through Charlottesville. Christmas wreaths hung bright and bold against simple household doors. Lights wrapped the trees, the glass glinting in the pale sunlight. No one was quite ready to give up Christmas. Humans walked through the town in bold, colored scarves and big practical boots. Laughter filled the air, and the cafes offered hot chocolate with extra marshmallows.

Festivity clung to the very fabric of the town, much like the coat of snow it wore. The roofs were patchy-white as though someone had sprinkled icing sugar over them. There was a feeling of peace to it, a quiet understanding that the world had paused for a few days to allow everyone to breathe.

Dorvu was not satisfied with the paltry snow that had fallen. His favorite students would return soon, and this wouldn't do. He wanted to do something to make them smile. The silver dragon swooped through the air, ignored the rabbits, and surveyed the lawns around the front of the school. He blew a great breath of cold air and transformed the school building into something from a Christmas card. Gone were the dark flashes of tile beneath the light snow, now replaced with a thick layer of pure white. The windows were frosted, and small silvery icicles hung from the flashing. It was a work of art, even if the dragon did think so himself.

———

The Blue Ridge mountains wore a thick white coat atop their peaks. Alison smiled as they came into view, her familiar response. The pale winter light gave the ridges a blue sheen that made them look almost otherworldly.

"No one told me if they got anything exciting for Christmas." Kathleen looked expectantly at the group. "Half the fun of Christmas is sharing your gifts."

Aya chewed her bottom lip. "My parents got me a gnome-made chess board. The pieces move themselves, and the rules are slightly different. It allows me to practice my magic and strategy."

"That sounds like wonderful fun." Emma beamed. "My aunt gave me some makeup. It changes depending on what outfit I'm wearing."

"You'll let me borrow some." Kathleen looked at her. "Won't you?"

Emma resisted the urge to roll her eyes.

"I left it at home. I'm keeping it for special occasions."

"The spring formal is a special occasion."

Kathleen took the formal dances very seriously. They were her chance to shine and show off her fashion know-how.

"Have you heard from that Christie girl?" Kathleen

looked at Alison. "She hasn't gotten into more trouble has she?"

Guilt filled Alison as she realized she hadn't told her friends about the darkness she saw emerge from the pendant.

She forced a bright smile. "No. I think she went back to London. I'm sure we'll see her in a few days. I hope her mom made a full recovery."

Kathleen sighed softly and nodded.

"Yes, I hope so too."

A weight settled over the group as they recalled the incident with the rogue shifter.

Peter grinned pointedly at the shifter. He gestured to the forest. "You'll have great fun running through this snow. It must feel amazing beneath your paws."

Luke relaxed. "Yeah, I'm looking forward to the first run of the year."

"Do you think they'll let us have champagne now that we're seniors?" Kathleen changed the topic. "Surely they won't mind one small glass."

"I don't really like champagne. It's too bitter for me," Emma admitted.

Kathleen leaned back in her seat, twisting the bracelet on her wrist. "You simply haven't had the good stuff."

"Well, they'll hardly give students Dom Perignon." Emma closed her eyes for a moment. "I don't see the fascination with it anyway. It's over-priced sparkly wine."

Kathleen had the good sense not to argue.

Alison reached between the seats and put her hand on Emma's shoulder. "Is everything okay?"

"I overheard my parents arguing about money," Emma whispered. "It's a sore point."

Kathleen held her bracelets in her lap, smiling at Emma, even as she stole a glance at the light bouncing off the stones.

Mrs. Beasley pulled the jitney to a stop outside the school's large gates.

"Now, don't cause too much trouble." She looked directly at Peter. "And don't blow anything up."

"I don't know why she looked at me. Ethan's far more prone to blowing things up than I am," he murmured as he stood.

Alison grinned. "I'm reasonably sure you're on equal footing. Although Ethan has his focus bands now."

Peter shook his head and exited the bus. His experiments did go wrong sometimes, but it really wasn't *that* frequently. His silver case stumbled from the luggage hold and rocked back and forth. He pushed it back onto its legs. The luggage circled before it set off toward the school, leaving him to jog along behind it.

"I give it five minutes before it blows up and throws his clothes everywhere." Luke smiled. "Anyone want to bet otherwise?"

Tanner laughed. "I won't go against a sure thing. You're on your own."

CHAPTER TWO

Alison felt as though the afternoon flew by. Everyone abandoned their luggage in their rooms and gathered in an empty classroom where they could speak freely. Dorvu had spent the time adding puffs of snow onto the school. The dragon gave them a toothy grin from the lawn as the sun set and slipped away for the evening.

As the temperature dropped, they retired to the study hall where the large open fires crackled. Flames licked at chopped logs, and small sparks occasionally popped and landed on the slate surround. Alison focused on watching the blaze slowly consume the wood. It relaxed her in a meditative way.

Tanner held her close with an arm around her waist. Luke remained near them while Kathleen and Aya sat at the edge of the group. When they began talking about fashion, the shifter sighed. After the rogue incident, he knew there was a chance he would be seen differently, but he had hoped that the bonds of friendship were stronger than that.

Peter grinned at him. "Don't worry. They'll come around soon enough. So, I thought I could do something to help the pack—"

Luke narrowed his eyes. "I am not risking my pack with one of your robots."

"No, not a robot. I thought more along the lines of cell phones, so you could talk to each other while in wolf form."

His companion raised an eyebrow. "We can communicate in wolf form."

"Oh." Peter looked away, then returned a grin. "Well, not to worry, I have a number of other projects I'm eager to try out."

Tanner looked at him. "Have you decided which colleges to apply to? I'm still not sure, and time's running out."

Alison frowned. "I thought you'd decided?"

"No, I'm not sure what I want to do. You plan to be a bounty hunter like your dad, right?"

"I want to do criminal psychology, but I'll see if I can do a minor in musical theatre."

"You can sing and dance the criminals into custody?" Peter saw the unamused expression on her face and rubbed the back of his neck. "Or, erm… Good luck with that. I'm sure it'll be awesome."

Tanner looked undecided. "I thought about doing sports science, or maybe medicine, but I'm not sure if I can get my math grade up enough to be accepted into medical school. And do I want to be surrounded by death and illness?"

"What would make you happy?" Alison put her hand on

his thigh. "This is your future. You need to be happy in your path."

He looked pointedly at Peter and Ethan. "Don't laugh at me for being a dork, but I think I really want to be a professor here. But Xander Powell will never leave."

"I think you'd make a fantastic professor." She grinned. "You could teach the defense against dark magic or maybe the biology of magical beings. Maybe at that school in San Francisco and become a Sand Piper fan for their Louper team."

"Dark magic would be pretty badass," Ethan commented.

"It does have a ring to it," Tanner admitted.

"I'm going into law." Luke glanced at Kathleen, waiting for her to sneer. "I want to be a defense attorney with a focus on family law. I want to help kids out of bad situations."

Peter smiled. "I'll do journalism with a minor in business. I'm not entirely sure whether I'll focus on journalism or running a business combining magic and tech yet. I guess I'll see when I get there."

Alison couldn't help but wonder what Izzie's plans were. She couldn't attend college, or at least not stay on campus. Tanner squeezed her shoulder and kissed her temple.

"I'm sure she's having adventures and is completely fine."

Luke's heart ached for Izzie. He felt like he needed her company and reassurances more than ever. A part of him had understood the rogue shifter's desire to fit into society and be seen as an equal instead of a mutt. That simple truth terrified him.

The kitchen pixies outdid themselves for the New Year's celebration. There weren't many students there, but the magical team had gone out of their way to make sure those who were brought the New Year in with a bang.

A myriad of tiny white lights twinkled from the ceiling like stars against the night sky. White silk snowflakes cascaded down the walls, and white and silver lace cloths bedecked the tables. The few occupied tables held center-pieces of unique glass artwork. Alison and her friends had a design of interconnected snowflakes and a small castle covered in a thick layer of snow. It shimmered blue and purple under the dimmed lights overhead.

The pixies had spent all afternoon cooking up a storm. A veritable feast appeared on the plates, starting with a small fresh salmon starter drizzled with fresh dill sauce.

"I never knew salmon could taste this good." Emma savored the last bite. "I swear they're spoiling us."

The main course was beef wellington with perfectly roasted potatoes, carrots, and a rich gravy.

"They should put this gravy in a cup, so I can drink it," Ethan declared as he eyed his empty plate. "Do you think they'd do that for me?"

A kitchen pixie with a severe spiked haircut appeared at his side. "No, I would not. Although I might be convinced to give you a larger piece of dessert." She smiled.

It was always nice to have your hard work appreciated.

Dessert was an indulgent chocolate cake served with the creamiest vanilla ice-cream Alison had ever tasted.

Luke leaned back in his chair. "I'll never walk again. I might have to roll to my room later."

"I don't know. I think I could fit an extra slice of that cake in." Ethan looked hopefully in the direction of the staff. "It was really good."

The pixies chatted with the headmistress and ignored him entirely.

***

Mara waited for the right time to approach Alison with the note and gift she had received from Izzie at Christmas. Her heart had lightened upon seeing the familiar handwriting. She had worried about the girl. It was difficult to be on the run and hide during Christmas, which should be a time of joy and family.

Xander looked meaningfully at her, and Mara nodded. Alison deserved to know, and there were so few students around that she could risk handing it to her there in the hall. She was sure the kitchen pixies wouldn't say a word to anyone.

***

Alison looked up when the headmistress approached their table with a small brown parcel and a note. She said nothing but desperately hoped it was something from Izzie. Christmas had been full of happiness, but she missed her best friend.

Mara walked around the table and smiled as she handed Alison the items.

"Our mutual friend managed to get this to me. I do hope that it brightens your celebrations."

Alison opened the envelope, looking calmer on the outside than she felt. It held two notes. She handed Luke the one with his name on it and read hers over twice. A flood of relief filled her at Izzie's adventures and the fun she was having.

She had traveled extensively. They rarely stayed in one place for very long but had seen the most amazing things. She had experienced magic that she had no idea existed before, and the worlds were far bigger than she'd imagined. The people pursuing them got close a few times, but they managed to slip away without too much trouble. Izzie spoke about coming into her own magic, and she couldn't wait to sit down and talk to her friend face to face. Alison noticed how carefully she worded everything and the way she hid the details so that no one could find her.

Luke read his note with a goofy smile on his face. Alison was pleased to see the shifter look relaxed for the first time since he'd got back to the school. Kathleen and Aya had pushed him away because of what he was. Part of her didn't blame them for their wariness, but he was still their friend.

Alison opened the brown-wrapped parcel and found a beautiful little telescope with another note inside.

"For your midnight walks. We will look at the same stars most nights."

She removed her glasses carefully and placed them on the

table so she could see the thin veil of magic that encircled the telescope. The spell connected them and allowed her to feel what her friend felt. She ran a fingertip slowly down the deep-blue length of the device and felt flickers of Izzie's joy.

"Thank you, Miss Berens."

The headmistress smiled.

"It's not long until midnight."

With that, she returned to the small gathering of professors.

"How is she?" Tanner gestured to the note. "Is she okay?"

"She's having an amazing time. You'd never know she's running for her life." Alison laughed.

Ethan smiled sadly. "That sounds like Izzie. She always had a way to find the adventure in life. I'm glad she's doing well."

Jason sat at a small table as far away from Alison and her friends as he could. He hadn't really tasted the food or participated in the conversation with his new roommates. The headmistress had made sure he was assigned to a group of seniors who were skilled at magic, but were recent transfers.

His thoughts focused on the state of his life and how he would proceed. He had the semester to find a way to free himself from the ties to dark magic.

It would take more than a few short months to atone for everything he'd done, but he had a long life ahead of him—or so he hoped. First, he needed to prove to himself and those around him that he was sincere.

———

"What's Jason doing here?" Emma nodded in his direction, scrunching up her nose as if she could smell sour milk. "I thought he spent as much time with his rich, dark magic family as possible."

Luke's lip curled up in a snarl.

"I have no idea, but I bet it's no good."

Alison glanced at him. His magic and soul had shifted colors. There was something softer about him and a spark of hope she hadn't seen before. "Something is different… maybe."

Still, she remained suspicious. Without him, so much of the destruction from last year might not have happened.

The loud dong of a bell filled the air, and a glass of sparkly golden liquid appeared at each table setting. They stood and raised their glass as the pixies counted down to midnight.

An explosion of fireworks arced across the ceilings. Vibrant flashes of gold, red, and blue burst from the darkness as rockets flew up the walls and exploded in shocks of color and noise. Delicate fireworks were interspersed between them in slower-moving hues that cascaded down the walls and disappeared. The display ended when a huge multi-colored star bloomed in the center of the ceiling and spread outward to the four corners.

Small scrolls appeared on the tables, and the pixies wore expressions of smug happiness. The students sat and exchanged glances. "We all open them at the same time," Alison said.

They untied the sky-blue ribbons on their delicate scrolls and unraveled them. Tanner burst into laughter when he read his fortune.

Alison leaned over to read it and laughed.

"Well, share," Kathleen smirked. "You shouldn't keep good things to yourself."

"A closed mouth gathers no feet," Tanner said, unable to keep a straight face.

Everyone laughed. "I didn't think you were that bad." Emma smiled. "Mine said 'she who appreciates pixies will have a prosperous year.'"

"Mine said 'hard work pays off in the future, laziness pays off now.'" Ethan frowned. "I'm not sure how to take that."

Alison smiled at him. "I think if you work hard and get your grades up, you'll do well. Your grades are improving, so it sounds like encouragement."

"How accurate are these fortunes anyway?" Kathleen put hers down. "Because I think mine is wrong or broken."

"How could it be broken?" Tanner laughed.

She pushed her scroll away. "Well, it says, 'when you get something for nothing, you merely haven't been billed for it yet,' which really sounds stupid to me. Sometimes, people give gifts."

Alison and Emma shared a look but said nothing.

Mara covered her mouth as she tried to restrain the

laughter at her fortune. The pixies had clearly had a lot of fun with them this year. She held it out to Xander to read.

"Only trust fortune scrolls for fortune telling. All other methods are inferior."

Xander laughed and admired her bright smile. It had been a long and hard year, and he was glad to see her back to her old self, even if for a moment. He'd worried that the New Year's celebration would be hard on her with Izzie away and the school so quiet, but it seemed to have done her good.

Ira had been reserved throughout the meal. Xander had noted that the new professor hadn't made much of an effort to integrate himself with his colleagues. He had rejected all invitations outside of school activities and disappeared at odd hours. If he didn't know better, Xander would have thought he was a shifter who needed to run.

Lucy smiled at Ira. "How are you finding your New Year's?" She tried to brush her unruly mane of red hair out of her face. "Do the students treat you well enough?"

"Yes, the students are very polite and receptive. I must admit I hadn't expected quite so much enthusiasm from them for a class on magic and mechanics." He took a sip of the elf wine. "The number of female students was entirely unexpected."

Xander doubted that very much. Ira was a handsome young man in his late twenties who turned heads wherever he went. His bright green eyes and dark, almost pitch-black hair were model-perfect. He was much like Xander had been at that age, capable of having any woman he chose and perfectly willing to take advantage of it.

Lucy sipped her wine. "The students are very open-minded, and many are quite eager to blend magic with human technology. They are our future. I do wish they would stop making dents in my ceiling, though. I don't know how they manage to turn harmless potions into volatile pastes, but they do it time and again."

"They certainly keep us on our toes," Mara agreed.

Xander looked at Alison and her friends. "Life would be boring if they were all well-behaved and did exactly as they were told. Chaos and experimentation often come with great potential. How else will they learn?"

Jason was ready to retire from the celebrations for the evening, but he opened his fortune scroll.

'A window of opportunity won't open itself.'

He frowned. The kitchen pixies wrote the fortunes, and he wasn't sure how much truth was in their words. They had magic, of course, but whether that included a minor seer's ability was the real question. He looked at Alison and her friends laughing and enjoying the evening. At that moment, he envied her. He had given up chances at real friendships in the hope of climbing his dark magic family's social ladder. *Even that didn't work.* He felt the pain in the center of his chest again. *I can do better.*

He folded the fortune carefully and slipped it in his pocket. It would be a reminder when he felt weak and the desire to return to the darker path tempted him. He gave a shudder at the thought that it was even possible.

"We should go to the kemana tomorrow. We can make a day of it. Explore, you know," Ethan proposed, playing with his focus bands.

Kathleen grinned. "That sounds great. I have some Christmas money left, and I'd love to see what bargains I can pick up."

"I wouldn't mind wandering." Luke stretched to shake off the stiffness that came with sitting for a long period. "They have the best burgers down there."

"Do you always think of your stomach? There is more to life than food, you know." Emma couldn't keep the smile from her face.

"I know. There's Louper and running." Luke grinned.

"A simple life for a simple boy," Kathleen said.

Luke narrowed his eyes and debated whether it was worth allowing his wolf side forward.

"We can't all be magpies chasing pretty baubles." Alison smiled at him. "Some of us prefer experiences over material goods."

Aya stood. "It's late. Maybe we should head to bed. We don't want to miss breakfast. I heard the pixies are preparing something memorable to celebrate the first day of the year. I'd like to start it off right."

CHAPTER THREE

The pixies prepared rainbow unicorn pancakes full of edible glitter and smooth chocolate sauce for breakfast. The friends ate and headed to the kemana in high spirits and with a feeling that everything was as it should be.

Tanner slid his arm around Alison's waist.

"Is there anything in particular you'd like to see?" he asked as they stepped off the bottom of the winding staircase. "I'm happy to be around the magic and see what we stumble across."

She smiled as the kemana's magic washed over her. "Wandering around sounds good, and maybe practicing our magic. I think I'd like to work with mine a little."

Ethan ran his thumb over his focusing bands and called his magic as he glanced at the familiar stalls and shops. The place was quieter than usual. Most people were still home for the festive season. He focused and formed a small white orb which floated before him. The bright lights around them meant he didn't need one, but it was a simple spell. A nice starting point to find his feet.

Kathleen stepped away and looked slowly between the sphere and the focusing bands on his wrist. The glow gradually condensed into a fairy light that bounced above head height. He grinned, feeling that he could finally control his ability.

They started down the street without too much attention to their surroundings. They had all day to shop, and in that moment, they wanted to explore their magic.

Aya held her hand out in front of her, and bright, orange flames emerged from her teal-colored shirt to coat her lower arm.

Emma went to extinguish them, but Aya stepped back and turned them to hot-pink.

"Touch them."

Peter reached out slowly, and a look of bemusement filled his face.

"There's no heat." He ran his fingers through them as they turned green. "Why is there no heat?"

Aya grinned. "I've practiced my glamours. I thought they might be useful."

"That's a glamour?" Ethan poked the tip of a flame and laughed. "That is so cool."

Kathleen sniffed and held her hand out palm-up. Her brow scrunched in concentration as she called upon her magic. Not one to be out-done, she formed a small fireball in her palm.

"I recommend against poking this one." She smirked. "I only play with the real thing."

Aya rolled her eyes.

"You can't help yourself," Emma muttered.

The fireball grew from golf ball to apple size and larger still. Kathleen closed her hand around it, and the flames flickered between her clenched fingers and grew even more. A wood elf watched from his stall with narrowed eyes. "You had best not burn my shop down."

Alison walked to Kathleen and engulfed the growing fire with an energy wall.

"If you worked a little harder to refine your spells rather than show off, I wouldn't need to save you from yourself quite so often." Alison pulled her magic back.

"Oh, really." Kathleen stood taller. "It's happened once."

Tanner looped his arm around Alison's waist. "Why don't we keep moving?"

Luke felt uncomfortable as he watched his friends play with their magic. It was a reminder that he was different. Peter nudged him with an elbow. "Come on, wolfie. Let's go and find something interesting."

Luke snorted at the name. Peter led him down a narrow walkway between stalls, and the shifter allowed himself to relax and enjoy their surroundings. The fashion and jewelry shops of the main pathway down the heart of the kemana were now replaced by more boutique shops.

Peter had no idea where he was going, but he knew that it was a bad idea for Luke to stay around Kathleen after she had been embarrassed. She would take her humiliation out on him, and she had already hurt him by shunning him.

They made their way past specialty bookstores, one of which was devoted entirely to fairy history. Luke slowed and peered into the small window, but the fairy inside fluttered her wings and almost shooed him away.

"I don't care about the fairies' history anyway. Shifters are far more interesting," Luke grumbled as he turned his focus elsewhere.

They stopped at a food stall selling a mix of freshly cooked meats in sauces packed full of spices that Luke couldn't identify. He chose a small selection and bit into a strip of deep purple meat dipped in something pale green. His eyes went wide as the spices burned his tongue and his throat dried.

Peter laughed and passed him a bottle of a pale-blue liquid. Luke gasped and drank half in one long gulp. He didn't notice the fresh elderflower flavor or the slightly syrupy texture, only sweet relief from the spices that he was positive had stripped his taste buds away.

"Shouldn't you be able to smell the burn with your super senses and all?" Peter asked, taking the rest of the offensive meat from him.

"It doesn't work like that. I didn't know the smell, so I didn't know what it did." Luke ran his tongue over his teeth.

"Now you know." Peter grinned.

They continued their walk, noting the changing surroundings. The stalls and shops slowly gave way to mature trees with broad boughs and dark, knotty trunks and numerous vines. The bright colors of the ceiling faded into the thick, verdant canopy. Peter summoned a pair of small orbs to compensate for the lower light levels.

Small cottages of interwoven branches and creepers sprouted up around them.

"Druids." Peter looked around. "I think we found the druid quarter."

There was a quiet peace about the area that soothed Luke's soul in a way only running with his pack ever could. He breathed deep and caught the scent of fresh, damp dirt and the almost spring-like smell of new growth.

Shops nestled between the trees, manned by long-haired people wearing natural colors and flora in their hair. They greeted the boys with bright smiles that reached their leafy-toned eyes.

"And what brings you here today?" an older woman asked.

Luke shrugged. Her selection of charms seemed mostly to help plants grow and minor healing spells.

Nothing appealed to either Luke or Peter, but it was fun to wander and see something new. The druids watched them closely from the foliage and security of their cottages. Thin vines twitched behind the boys, setting Luke's nerves on edge. He could hear the rustling of their leaves against the floor and walls.

An older Druid woman looked at him. "Stay true to who you are, wolf. Do not forsake your nature for others."

An image of the rogue played in his mind, and he glared at the woman. He would never turn from his pack or his wolf side. Being a shifter wasn't perfect, but it was who and what he was.

Peter ran his fingers over a deep-green vine with white heart-shaped leaves.

"Be careful. Not everything should be touched," a pretty young girl called, stepping out of the shadows.

Her black hair fell in soft waves down to her waist. To Peter, it looked almost like feathers in the light through the canopy overhead. As she walked, her appearance seemed overlaid with avian rather than entirely human. The sense endured only for the blink of an eye, leaving him trying to remember if he'd read anything about beings like that.

She gestured to the vine. "Our world may look lush and green, but some things are rather dangerous."

"Will he be okay?" Luke stepped closer to his friend. "Has he been poisoned?"

"Not yet." The girl smiled. "But if he continues to run his hands over everything, he will be."

Luke's protective instincts kicked in. "Is that a threat?"

She tilted her head slightly, a small furrow forming between her brows. "No."

"Come, Ilana. There are duties to carry out." An older woman ushered the girl into a cottage. "My apologies. Please enjoy our wares."

Luke eyed the vine. "Do you want to head back? I'm not sure we're welcome here."

"No, we've never been here before, and they've all been nice."

They continued down the twisting pathway and deeper into the forest-like neighborhood. Tiny, delicate white flowers grew from the gaps in a larger cottage on Luke's left. Small windows held a faint yellow glow, and the scent of honeysuckle and roses filled the air. His feet carried him toward the cottage. He was almost at the door when an older druid with grey streaks in his dark hair grabbed his shoulder.

"That's not for you. Time to return to your friends, young shifter." He turned Luke back in the direction he'd come.

Luke looked longingly at the cottage before he quickly

followed Peter. He'd come back and find out what intrigued him about the place. It called to him, and he wasn't one to ignore his curiosity.

Alison and the others had chosen an unfamiliar street in search of something truly special. Kathleen stopped at the fourth jewelry store of the day and looked inside at the shiny trinkets. She pursed her lips and sighed.

"They don't have what I'm looking for."

"What are you looking for?" Emma asked, perusing the rings. "Maybe we can help,"

"I don't know yet." She turned away. "I'll know it when I see it."

Tanner and Ethan shared a frustrated look but said nothing. Kathleen was already volatile after Alison had to control her fire.

"Why don't you form some badass wings?" Ethan grinned at her. "Show us how it's done."

Tanner squeezed her hip gently, a small touch of reassurance against the increasing peer pressure.

Alison smiled. In this quieter part of the kemana, she felt more comfortable showing the full extent of her Drow side. Her magic came so easily down there. It flowed into her fingers like a cool stream. *Wings*, she said to herself. The image of small feathered wings formed in her mind, and she focused and mentally pressed her magic into the shape.

To everyone's delight, oil-black feathers appeared on her back. They expanded into a pair of small, delicate wings. Alison flapped them lazily a few times to show they worked.

"No." Tanner glared at Kathleen. "She won't try to fly."

Alison gave him a warning look before she grounded the magic and the appendages vanished in a soft puff of black smoke.

Tanner smiled in response. "I didn't want her pressuring you. She's already in a pushy mood."

Before she could speak, he pressed his finger gently to her lips. "I know you can look after yourself, but would it kill you to let me look after you a little?"

She smiled and relaxed. As long as he didn't try to fight her battles for her, she could allow a little protectiveness here and there.

Kathleen had already marched off, leaving everyone to decide whether to leave her to her own devices or follow her.

Ethan pointed down a street they hadn't seen before. "I vote we turn left. Kathleen went straight ahead."

"I'm with Ethan. Let her stew and get her head straight," Emma stated.

"Looks like it's decided." Tanner smiled. "Anyone want to go after Kathleen?"

Silence was the only response.

They passed small elven and wand shops. The temperature of the air began to increase, and the light around them shifted to a slightly orange hue. They followed the natural bend in the road and found themselves in a new neighborhood.

Every surface seemed ablaze. Bright orange flames flickered and danced along the edges of the street. Small blue and orange tongues of fire licked at the exteriors of cottages and shops that seemed hewn from rocks.

"Ifrit." Alison looked around in awe. "I think we found the Ifrit quarter."

Aya took a step back. "Aren't they dangerous? Is it a good idea to be here?"

Alison took Tanner's hand. The heat wasn't unbearable. It was more like a warm summer's day. The scent of burning wood and jasmine filled the air.

"It can't be so bad, and we know how to defend ourselves if needed," she said, peering into a shop window.

The store contained everything a fire-worker could ever wish to own. Alison studied the blood-red and lava-orange gems and crystal figurines. A small salamander figurine caught her eye. The creature blinked, and Alison smiled as its tongue passed over its lips.

Ethan pointed at it as he walked closer. "Did you see it move? Is it alive?"

"I'm not sure. It might be enchanted to move a little." Alison went to the shop door. "Let's find out, shall we?"

The rest of the group were more apprehensive but followed her into the warm shop's interior. A pair of Ifrit stood behind a black stone counter, watching the students with dark-red eyes.

Alison smiled at them. "Good morning. We were curious about your salamander."

The Ifrit were tall beings with vibrant manes of flames instead of hair and small black horns in the place of human eyebrows. Their angular features resembled humans, but their fingers looked slightly longer than was entirely normal. They dressed in a mix of charred blacks and vivid oranges, the loose, flowing garments moving almost like the flames around them.

"Which salamander?" the Ifrit asked, moving to the window. "We have three."

Tanner leaned in, whispering to Alison. "Be careful. Ifrit are tricksters and very fond of semantic games."

She nodded quickly in understanding.

The Ifrit retrieved the trio from the window. The first was an orange crystal lizard with small black spots down the center of its back. It walked lazily up the Ifrit's arm, while the black stone one with bright orange toes and tipped tail walked along its hand and glared at Alison. It was the third, whose body resembled flames bound into a solid form, that held her attention. The fire swirled across its back and raced up and down its tail.

"We can strike a good bargain. I can see you have many things to exchange," the Ifrit told her, holding the fire salamander a little closer.

Tanner saw the hunger in his eyes when he looked at Alison's white hair. She peered over her glasses and saw the blood-red sparks of ill intent in the Ifrit's soul and gave him a polite smile.

"Thank you, but not today." She turned away.

The black stone salamander hopped off the Ifrit's hand and landed on the balsamic-black floor, blending in almost entirely. It scurried after the students as they exited the shop and turned toward the heart of the kemana.

"Kathleen must have calmed down by now." Emma glanced at the others. "I'm sure she'll be at the crepe place."

Alison sensed someone or something following them. She looked back over her shoulder but saw nothing. The streets were still mostly empty when they returned to the more well-traveled areas.

The small salamander stopped when the light grew brighter and the elf population increased. The Ifrit controlling the lizard was sure that the Drow would return, and when she did, he would take a small piece of her magic for his own.

The group reunited at their favorite shop. Everyone indulged in large crepes filled with sugar, cream, and chocolate. Luke and Peter shared a table with Alison and Tanner. Kathleen and Aya didn't look at the shifter, but Kathleen hadn't made any comments, so Luke took that as a win.

Once they'd finished, Alison looked around the group.

"Where now?"

"Wait, is that Professor Heineken?" Kathleen pointed at a handsome, dark-haired man outside. "I think it is."

"We should go and say hi." Emma pushed her seat back.

"Oh, come on, he's not that hot." Ethan gestured at him. "Besides, he's a professor."

Kathleen shrugged and smirked. "I won't be a high school student much longer."

"We can't let her corner him." Tanner left a tip for the waitress. "He won't stand a chance."

They exited and saw Kathleen fluttering her eyelashes at the clearly uncomfortable professor. He was young, perhaps his late twenties, but still far too old for Kathleen.

"We haven't seen you in the kemana before." She

chewed her bottom lip. "Maybe we can offer you some pointers?"

Professor Heineken frowned. "I think I can manage, thank you."

"What brings you here?" Tanner smiled. "Post-Christmas shopping?"

The professor put his hands in his pockets. "Er, yes. It's the best time to pick up some bargains. I should be going."

He walked briskly away before anyone could ask anything else. Alison watched his retreat and wondered why he headed toward the shadier part of the kemana. He could be confused in his rush to escape Kathleen, but Brownstone had taught her to be suspicious.

CHAPTER FOUR

I ra glanced furtively over his shoulder to make sure he wasn't followed. He felt as though the students had ambushed him, though they couldn't know anything. That would be ridiculous. No, he was merely paranoid, he told himself. The kemana beneath the school was very different from the others he had visited. There was more color and vibrancy that he hadn't noticed elsewhere. He pushed the thought aside and decided he was more aware of this one because he intended to use the crystal.

The shop owners and other patrons paid him no attention. His jeans and slate-gray sweater blended in well with the students. Ira used that to his advantage, slipped between a pair of magical artifact stores, and emerged in an unsavory area. Every kemana had somewhere darker and ill-maintained where people gathered for illicit reasons.

The dirty street and the old blood stains made him feel he was doing something wrong. The contact he'd found had insisted on meeting there, though. Ira had pushed for a nice coffee shop in Charlottesville, but the man was adamant it had to be in these shadows.

The space was small and backed by several shops. The residents no doubt ignored what happened there. A small shard of bone jutted from beneath the wooden wall of the bookstore. Ira called his magic and felt the comfort of knowing he could defend himself should the need arise. It wouldn't be the first time things had gone awry. He'd had to flee the country when he'd tried this experiment in Canada.

He paced, waiting. "This time is different. I'm better prepared."

"Talking to yourself?" a gruff voice asked.

Ira turned more slowly than his instincts demanded. He wasn't willing to show surprise.

"Melchior?"

The tall, reedy man stepped into the dim light. A deep scar ran from his left temple and cut across his eye to the cheekbone.

"You must be Mr. Heineken." He circled Ira. "I didn't expect someone so...clean-cut."

Ira's magic flickered in the palm of his hand, eager to be used.

"Do you know what you're asking?" Melchior stopped near the bone shard. "The price has gone up."

"No deal. We had an agreement. I have other options." Ira started to walk away.

Melchior nudged the bone shard with his foot. "No, you don't. I made sure of it."

Ira ran his options through his mind. He couldn't leave the school before the final semester, and he knew this particular crystal was the easiest to access and the most likely to fit his purposes.

He turned to face Melchior "What is the new price? I may still walk away."

The man fixed him with a cold glare. "You owe me a favor—any favor—whenever I choose to call it in. And that little stone you always carry."

Ira fought to control himself. The stone was an elemental summoning stone, his sixteenth birthday gift and the only thing he had left of his brother. He carried it everywhere with him. Seth had died because he had been dragged into the wrong company. Ira needed this experiment to proceed smoothly so he could avenge his brother.

"No deal."

Melchior sneered. "You don't have a choice."

A brawny pair of shifters stepped into view, blocking the only exit.

"Take the deal, Mr. Heineken, so we can all move on with our day."

Ira rolled the stone in the palm of his hand. It was all he had left.

As the shifters edged closer, their jaws sprouted sharp lupine teeth. Ira straightened his spine. He was doing this for Seth. Those who killed him would suffer.

He held the small coral-colored stone out to Melchior.

"And one favor at a time of my choosing." The man took the stone. "Don't forget."

"Can we kindly move to the crystal now?"

Ira clenched his fists and barely held his anger in check. Everything about him was tight and tense, but he knew better than to try to fight his way out of the situation. The shifters stepped aside and allowed him passage to the main area of the kemana.

Melchior patted him on the back.

"Everything is ready. It'll be a nice easy procedure."

Ira resisted the urge to step away from the other man. Melchior's reputation preceded him, and it included a lot of blood and broken bones. Neither appealed to Ira.

The kemana was oddly quiet. A few smaller shops were closed with neat wooden shutters over their doors and windows. Shifters and witches lurked in the shadows, watching as Melchior walked like a king surveying his kingdom.

Ira reminded himself that he was doing this for Seth.

The crystals in the kemanas always produced a feeling of absolute awe in him. He had seen a number across America and Canada, and the reaction remained the same every time. Normally, people would be nearby, looking at the crystal and meandering around the underground city. Now, there was no one.

"Come along, Mr. Heineken. Time is money." Melchior looked pointedly at the crystal. "And I'm not sure you can afford more of my time."

Ira gritted his teeth and said nothing as he retrieved a small vial. He needed a tiny sample to see if it was a good fit. It had taken him five long years to learn how to draw magic from the kemana crystals. A scar on the heel of his left hand was a reminder of the first time he had tried and the power had been too much. It had bitten into his flesh and driven him away.

He quieted his mind and allowed his magic to slip into his hands. Slowly, he walked forward and pressed the power against the crystal, seeking a suitable access point. Melchior watched him closely, distracting him. Ira needed to get it over and done with. He found a slight weakness and siphoned a vestige of magic into the vial.

The vessel glowed a bright white-blue which was difficult to hide. He slipped it into a leather pouch and into his pocket.

Melchior smiled, a savage expression on his face. "I look forward to your next visit, and don't forget that favor you owe me."

Ira could never forget. It meant he was tied to Melchior and in the man's pocket. There were very few worse places to be.

CHAPTER FIVE

K athleen led the way through the dining hall. The students and professors had all returned by now. Alison pursed her lips and wished she could weave a small spell to quiet the cacophony of sound a little.

"Christmas was amazing. The flight back to London was so long, though, and I had the worst stopovers. I had to try to sleep on one of those awful couches in Germany. The airport's really creepy when they're closed for the night. The Germans were nice, but they're really into their efficiency, aren't they? We didn't get any snow, but you don't expect any in London. I mean, you'll probably get some in January, but everyone knows Christmas will be wet and gray." Alison wondered how Christie managed to pack so many words into one breath.

The younger girl continued to talk to her new friends who listened with rapt attention. Alison smiled. She must have gotten the pendant to her mum and saved her. Guilt filled Alison as she realized she still hadn't told her friends about the darkness that emerged from the pendant. She wasn't intentionally hiding it from them but hadn't found the right moment to bring it up.

Breakfast was particularly generous that morning. The kitchen pixies fluttered between the tables. "Remember, this is the most important meal of the day. You have to be awake and ready for your classes," she said as Peter tried to shove the last of his croissant into his mouth while reading an essay.

"This Blackwell guy seems to think that copper is more suitable to magic weavings when combining magic with technology, but copper is so expensive. I've tried to use aluminum, but the magic bounces off half the time." The pixie frowned and crossed her arms when Peter missed his mouth and dropped crumbs everywhere. "I really feel we should be able to do more with steel. People have ignored it in favor of the fashionable materials and those mentioned in the older alchemical texts."

"What about materials from Oriceran. Wouldn't they be suitable?" Ethan asked.

"Oh, don't encourage him," Kathleen huffed. "He'll never stop talking about it."

Peter ignored her. "Cost is the problem again." He brushed crumbs off his uniform. "I'm a poor student after all."

"Do we have dark magic or potions first?" Emma pushed her chair back. "Dark magic, right?"

"No, potions." Tanner glanced at Peter's essay. "We're doing offense and defense this semester."

"No more tedious healing potions?" Kathleen smoothed her hand over her hair. "I can't believe they made us wait until the final semester to do something interesting and worthwhile."

Emma frowned. "Healing potions are worthwhile. They can make the difference between life and death in a fight."

"I've heard the fashion world is vicious." Ethan grinned and made a cat-claws gesture. "You might need those healing potions."

Everyone but Kathleen laughed as they headed toward the potions lab.

"I can't believe this is our final semester," Aya commented, side-stepping a freshman reading a book and entirely oblivious to the world around her. "It's so weird."

"It's amazing. We'll be free soon," Kathleen exclaimed.

Alison wasn't sure it would be quite as simple as that. She looked forward to a new and interesting degree of freedom and exploring the world, but she didn't expect sunshine and rainbows.

Tanner tensed as Jason Parker neared their little group and followed them to the potions lab. They hadn't spoken a word to him since his return. Jason's role in the fight at the end of Junior year was well known. As far as Tanner was concerned, Jason had made his allegiances very clear, and they weren't to the school or him and his friends.

Jason was keenly aware of the way the other students looked at him and their judgment. Just like he was aware of how most of his bloodline had disowned him and blamed him in part for all the death and destruction that had befallen them.

That turned out to be the break he needed to walk away without any backlash. They wanted him gone. He had wandered for a while, not sure what to do with himself, reduced to living in a shelter that catered to magicals.

But one day, Turner Underwood, the retired Fixer had showed up at the door and offered him a chance. "I have been rescuing your kind for hundreds of years," he had said. "What? You think my mission was to only rescue those magicals who deserved it? Would have made my job a lot easier. No... and I'm not here for those who need it necessarily, either. I'm here for those who want it. Get up, you're coming with me, unless your own plans are working out?"

Jason had scrambled to his feet, almost forgetting his wand and small bag of clothes he still had, and ran after Turner, grateful for the chance, any chance.

Months of listening to Turner's long stories and taking every direction from him, rising early and working hard all day had convinced Turner to talk to Mara Berens, putting the wheels in motion. At last, the invitation arrived.

Turner had leaned on his cane, his hands wrapped around the silver handle. "Of course, this is all up to you. But your time here is coming to a close. If you have another idea, take it." He had given Jason a wry smile, arching an eyebrow as he waited for the inevitable nod.

The school was Jason's only option still on the table. No other magical school would even consider taking him. Word had spread quickly through the magicals about what had happened at the School of Necessary Magic.

He shook his head and put the past away, the best he could, focusing on the present day and being back at school. *This is my last stop. I have to make it work.* He set his shoulders firmly and tried to ignore it. They had no idea what went on in his life away from school. Potions was his first class of the final semester. It wasn't his favorite, but he did well enough in it. The class gave him time to think. He needed to do something big to make a difference, but nothing had presented itself yet.

Professor Heineken walked down the hallway toward them, and Jason frowned. There was something a little off about him. The female students paid him a lot of attention, but Jason sensed something wrong beneath the surface. He made a mental note to dig into who the professor was and why he was at the school. It could be nothing, but it could be exactly what he needed. A chance at redemption.

Professor Fowler pulled her red mane into a tie, only for it to escape around her face again. She had tried a new conditioner on it, but her hair had a mind of its own and now stuck up even more creatively than it had before. The students filtered into the room, and she smiled broadly. The lab had been explosion-proofed over the break, which she hoped would help reduce the accidents they seemed prone to. She'd tried without success to figure out how they had managed to make the simple healing potion explode. It would forever be a mystery to her.

"Today, we will make a potion to remove someone's magic for an hour." She caught the excitement on a few faces. "Any student caught using this potion on *anyone* at the school will suffer severe consequences. It is not to be used as a prank. Do you understand?"

The students mumbled acknowledgment, and she continued, knowing that was the best she would get. She glanced at Alison, thinking the young Drow was the most likely to benefit.

"This is a complicated potion that requires your full attention. Only a small amount is needed to remove someone's magic. That makes it ideal to carry around in a small vial and use in a fight should you need it. You will make enough to use on one person. It can be used on artifacts and such as well. Given that it is ethically wrong to remove someone's magic to test your potions, you will use it on the crystals I'll hand out in a moment."

She set one pale-blue crystal from a small bag on each table around the lab. The students rolled them in their palms as they tried to determine what spell they contained. It was a small light spell she'd cooked up before breakfast that morning as there was no point in risking anything stronger.

"You'll work in pairs. The recipe is on the board at the front. Begin with your small copper cauldron and move into your silver-lined medium cauldron. Remember, this requires your absolute focus."

Professor Fowler looked over her shoulder and made sure the recipe was correct and clear.

"Well, go on, then."

Alison and Aya worked together near the back of the room.

"That does say wolfsbane, right? We put the wolfsbane in the lukewarm water and stir three times?" Aya frowned at the board. "I can't quite read her handwriting."

"I think it's willow herb, and the wolfbane goes into the medium pot when we have it boiling." Alison reread the recipe. "Adding the wolfsbane at the beginning will turn it into a poison."

"We're so screwed," Kathleen muttered to Emma. "Why can't she print it off or something?"

"Or give us a textbook to read it from," Emma responded as she measured out the willow herb. "Maybe we should say something to her."

Kathleen sighed. "It won't do any good. It's the last semester now, and it's only potions."

Alison watched as the potion slowly turned a pale purple in the warm water. It didn't seem quite right, but they had followed the recipe. Aya crushed the wolfsbane and silver dust together in the mortar and pestle.

Slowly, the lab took on the fresh green scent of spring. Unfortunately, a neon-green mist crept along the floor as well. Professor Fowler pursed her lips and studied it. She'd seen it when she'd made this potion before, but not at that density. Perhaps it was because they made so many at one time.

"Be sure that your wolfsbane and silver are thoroughly mixed and ground together, and it must be stirred counterclockwise." She circled the room, checking the students' progress.

To her surprise, Jason Parker's potion was exactly where it should be. The water had begun to thicken into a lavender-purple roux, and his wolfsbane was mixed beautifully with the silver. She didn't remember that he'd paid much attention in her class before, but she was happy to see him finally show his potential. Melissa and her partner's, on the other hand, had gone completely awry.

"No, stop. You'll have to start from the beginning." Professor Fowler held her hands over the cauldron to stop the girls from proceeding. "The wolfsbane must be mixed with the silver. What have you done here exactly?"

"Wolfsbane was added to the lime water, and willow herb was mixed with the slippery elm. That's what it says on the board."

Professor Fowler sighed. Perhaps her handwriting hadn't been quite as clear as she had initially thought.

"It was supposed to be willow herb in lukewarm water, and wolfsbane ground with silver." The professor picked up the small cauldron. "I'll dispose of this, and you can start again."

She scraped the thick ooze into her potion-proof bin and sealed the lid, leaving a note on top for the cleaners to be very careful and treat it as highly poisonous.

The other students had successfully deciphered her recipe and were mostly on the right path.

Professor Fowler handed a pestle to Kathleen. "The wolfsbane needs to be more thoroughly mixed with the silver than that. If you continue with that consistency, you'll produce a mild poison that will enrage them."

The redhead scowled at the pestle as though it had personally offended her before she resumed grinding the ingredients.

Once the potions were completed and moved into small ceramic bowls, Professor Fowler decided it was best to give verbal instructions.

"Take your pipette and half-fill it with the potion." She lifted her pipette to show them what she meant. "Then, drip three droplets slowly onto the crystal. Only three. If you have succeeded, the stone will turn a dark yellow color."

She watched the students closely. "Ethan, three drops only. Do not let that fourth drop hit the crystal."

He dropped the pipette back into the bowl and watched his crystal with narrowed eyes. To his and Peter's joy, it did turn a deep yellow color. They'd pulled it off.

Only one pair of students had failed, and their crystal turned a rather pretty rose-pink. It was a shame that it meant the crystal now contained a thread of bloodlust. Professor Fowler maintained her smile and reminded herself that it was only one crystal, and it wouldn't take her more than an hour to fix. At least nothing had exploded.

Professor Powell waited patiently for the students to settle. They ignored him and talked about their Christmas breaks. He exhaled slowly and calmed himself before he spoke in a loud, clear tone.

"Today, you will learn how to protect your mind." He waited until the hubbub quieted. "We have established that you can mostly protect your body, but your mind is rather important. For some of you at least."

That earned a laugh.

"Some less scrupulous magicians will attack a foe's mind. This can result in temporary issues such as blindness or hallucinations, or it can go further and turn a person mad or kill them."

Silence fell over the room. He had their attention now.

"You will learn two spells that you can weave in a fight situation to protect your minds. You'll work in pairs. One will attack, and one will defend. Then, you will switch places."

Alison listened intently. This was precisely the type of thing she needed to learn if she wanted to succeed as a bounty hunter. She paired off with Tanner and waited for Professor Powell's next instructions.

"The first spell requires clear visualization and control over your magic." He looked pointedly at the less-focused students. "If your visualization falters, the spell will disintegrate."

This spell had saved him from sticky situations in his younger years. It wasn't as powerful as the second spell or others in his arsenal, but it could give the user a few moments to think and retaliate.

"Summon your magic. You will require your purest magic. Visualize a clear bubble forming around your entire head. It should surround your head entirely. No weaknesses, no holes, no thin parts."

The students nodded.

"For the offensive, you will cast a minor confusion spell. Nothing too dangerous. Call upon your magic and whisper *mentem confundunt.* Do not press too hard and only say the spell once."

There was little chance of that offensive spell going too awry. At worst, it would make the victim feel a little drunk and lose balance. It was easy enough to remove if necessary but would wear off on its own within ten minutes.

"You cast the offensive spell first." Tanner lifted his wand and focused. "I'll try defensive."

Alison could feel the magic in her fingertips itching to be used. She gave him a moment before she whispered the words. The enchantment flowed out of her, and she saw the shift in Tanner's soul when it struck.

A frown deepened on his face as he focused on the image of a bubble. He could feel the confusion seeping into the edges of his thoughts, tugging his concentration away. The protection formed slowly and strengthened, resembling a soap bubble in his mind.

Alison smiled when she saw the confusion spell slip off Tanner's magic. He'd done it. She looked around the room and saw other students struggling. Ethan's magic was bound by a thin network of mustard-yellow lines where the confusion spell took hold. Concentration wasn't his strong point, even with his focus bands. He ran his fingers back and forth over them while he calmed his breathing, and slowly, the yellow mesh slipped away. A sheen of sweat had formed on his forehead, and he took a deep breath.

"You'll have to improve your focus, Ethan," Professor Powell chided.

The young man ignored him. He did the best he could and was aware of his flaws. Peter gave him an understanding smile before he sat a little taller in his seat and tried to form his own bubble.

Ethan's magic came much more easily since he'd practiced over Christmas. The focus bands had helped considerably. He ran the words over his tongue a few times to smooth the pronunciation before he spoke. To his alarm, the spell emerged stronger than he intended. He cursed under his breath and hoped his partner wouldn't be affected too badly.

Peter's bubble trembled in his mind's eye when the spell struck. He gritted his teeth and maintained protection as the enchantment slowly dripped off. He grinned, feeling really good about himself.

Professor Powell rubbed the spot between his eyebrows as he watched a pair of students almost fall off their chairs when their bubbles failed entirely. It was a simple spell. They didn't have a chance of moving onto something more complex if they couldn't form a bubble.

Jason was already familiar with these particular spells. Confusing someone gave you an edge in a fight, and he'd been taught to take every advantage he could get. Failing in his family usually got someone a magical backhand across the face. He had learned how to improve quickly and remember the lesson.

He hoped the professor's next pair would be of more use. In a fight, he needed more than to make the attacker feel intoxicated. Given his family affiliations, any fight he found himself in would carry large stakes, likely his life. He didn't have the time or patience to play around with meaningless enchantments.

Professor Powell separated the four students who struggled with the simple spell and moved them into a corner out of harm's way to practice.

"This next spell is more dangerous than the last, and the defense is thus stronger and more complicated. Once again, you need to form your magic in your mind but must speak the counter-spell at the same time. I know some of you struggle with multi-tasking, but now is a good time to learn."

Despite his warning, it would be easy enough to dispel it if necessary. They weren't ready for the truly dangerous ones, and he suspected only a handful of the students present ever would be.

"Those on the offensive will speak the words *sensus nebula*. This will remove your victim's senses for twenty minutes. They will be entirely deaf and blind and will be unable to feel magic or anything else that might help defense. Those caught under this spell are entirely vulnerable to every attack."

He smiled at the look of alarm on a few of the faces. At least they took it seriously.

"To defend against something this strong, speak the words *mentis perspicacia* and imagine a large shield extending from the ground to above your head. The aim is to create something resilient and large enough that the spell bounces off."

Ethan swallowed hard. Losing his senses sounded absolutely nightmarish. He wasn't sure he could visualize the defense with as much strength as was needed.

"You do offensive first." Peter smiled. "It'll give you time to get your head straight."

Ethan held his wand and spoke the complicated words, feeling his magic infuse them. Peter's eyes went wide when the spell struck. His shield hadn't formed entirely, and his sight faded immediately. The world around him sounded muffled as though he was underwater. He didn't know if completing his defense now would help, but it was his only chance. He squeezed his eyes shut and put everything he had into visualizing the protective layer in front of him. A bright red Centurion-style shield formed before him. He opened his eyes and could partially see. Everything was a haze, but the shield held.

"Peter, you need to react more quickly next time," Professor Powell said.

Alison was a natural with the offensive spell but found defense more of a challenge. The magic around her faded and she felt entirely lost. Everything looked bland and grey. She fought to form her shield and relaxed when the magic in her vision returned.

Kathleen lost all her senses and screamed. She'd thought of her future as a fashion icon rather than the shield. Everyone focused on her. Some sniggered, and others were horrified. Professor Powell pulled the spell from her. She tried to pretend that nothing had happened, but the red blush of humiliation didn't leave her cheeks for the rest of the class.

CHAPTER SIX

Jason saw his chance to do a little digging into the professor after dark magic class. Most of the other students spent the study period in the library. He was reasonably sure Professor Heineken was teaching a juniors class, which meant his office would be empty and unguarded. Jason put on his most charming smile and strolled up the winding stairs as though going to his dormitory, then cut left toward the professors' offices.

Professor Heineken's was at the very end with a small frosted glass window set into the dark wood door. His nameplate was engraved with swirling gold script. Jason quickly wove a stealth spell to quiet his steps and deflect attention should others see him. It wasn't perfect, but a full invisibility spell would take too long. He twisted the doorknob.

It was locked but that was no surprise. The professors didn't want students snooping in their private offices. Jason had come prepared, however, and retrieved his enchanted lock-picks. He smiled as he felt the soft thrum of magic within them. He was about to slip them into the slender lock when someone cleared their throat behind him.

Jason turned with an innocent expression on his face and a lie already formed. He hid the picks in his back pocket and looked at Professor Powell, the worst possible person to have caught him.

"Mr. Parker, what exactly do you think you're doing?"

"I was hoping to speak to Professor Heineken about technology in the magical world and how he came to focus on car mechanics."

Professor Powell raised an eyebrow and crossed his arms.

"And you thought that you'd surprise him by breaking into his office?"

"I thought I saw movement." Jason bit his bottom lip. "I was worried. After all the problems we've had at the school, I feared that something dark was here again."

Professor Powell exhaled through his nose. Jason knew he didn't believe a word of it.

"Given your history, Mr. Parker, I would expect you to be the origin of darkness there."

The words stung, but Jason maintained a calm expression.

"I have no reason to harm the professor. I was simply hoping to get some notes for an essay. Extra credit."

"Then come back when he's available. Don't let me see you here again. And in future, note that a stealth spell only makes people more suspicious of your intent."

Xander watched Jason leave and jog down the stairs. The boy was clearly up to something, but what? He peered through the window of Ira's office but saw no movement or shadows. The professor sighed and returned to his office and bigger problems. Small animals had shown up dead on the grounds, and no one knew why. He had a sneaking suspicion that it was very dark magic but needed to search his books for more information before he could act.

———

"Have you heard? Horace found a bunch of dead squirrels."

"Partridges, I heard."

"It's the dragon. He's probably stock-piling them for a cold snap or something."

Alison frowned when she overheard the conversation. She knew Dorvu ate anything he killed and wouldn't leave perfectly good meat for other animals to eat. The memory of the darkness escaping the pendant came to mind, and she shifted the weight of her bag on her shoulder. Glancing at her friends, she wondered when the right time would be to tell them.

They went to the library for study hall and found the gnomes had increased security since the missing books incident. In Alison's vision, a thick gold band encircled the floor. With her glasses on, she saw a very slight shimmer. The custodians were all on high alert and inspected every student's books on both the way in and out. Their poppies blew raspberries at everyone.

Librarian Leo Decker personally oversaw the extra security measures and ensured that every book had been double-tagged so that they would never be lost again. He'd drunk almost an entire bottle of whiskey when he found the missing books with bent spines and pages removed. Who would do such an awful thing?

He watched the young Drow girl sit at her usual table with her friends and force a smile as they discussed what had happened in the dark magic class. He didn't need Drow vision to see the weight on her shoulders.

"Have you heard about the dead animals?" Emma leaned forward. "They don't sound like Dorvu's work."

"What else could it possibly be? There aren't any predators on campus besides him," Kathleen remarked, pulling out her notebook.

"How did they die?" Alison hoped she sounded casual. "Does anyone know?"

Tanner wrapped his arm around her shoulders. "They look like they simply dropped dead. I guess it's the cold weather or something."

Alison knew it couldn't be that simple. They'd had deep snows before, and nothing like this had happened. What if it was the shadow thing from the pendant?

Luke joined them. His grin dropped the moment Kathleen and Aya deliberately moved away from him.

"I am nothing like him," Luke growled.

They hadn't told anyone what had happened in the woods that fateful day. He didn't dare specify what he was talking about, but everyone knew.

"You're a shifter." Kathleen refused to look at him. "Who knows what you're capable of?"

Peter grinned at Luke. "Fancy kicking my ass at elf chess later?"

"I've learnt a few new tactics over the holidays. We could play Drow versus light."

Peter leaned back and folded his arms. "Only if I play the Drow."

"Deal."

They both knew that Drow had the advantage, but Luke was happy to concede if it moved the topic from Kathleen's new view of him. He was glad to have Peter's support. Seeing the rogue had thrown him because he could understand how it all happened, and that scared him. If he didn't have his pack, would he be tempted to try something like that too?

CHAPTER SEVEN

Xander spent what time he could in his office, looking into possible causes of the dead animals. He feared that it was the Dark Mist from the World in Between that had hunted Leira Berens. Someone must have cast a death spell, and the mist had been pulled through to bring everything back into balance.

He walked the familiar path across the grass and crunched the frost underfoot. The dragon wheeled overhead, clearly enjoying himself as the sun set on the horizon. The snowcapped mountains took on a pink hue that softened their edges and caught Xander's eye. He paused for a moment to admire the scene and knew he was fortunate to have landed a position at the school. There were worse places in the world, and he'd seen many of them.

The sun continued its descent, and Xander continued his journey to Mara's cottage. Out of respect, it wasn't somewhere he visited often, but he needed her to understand that he wasn't behind the deaths. She would think of his past, and it didn't take much to jump to conclusions.

Horace scooped up a squirrel corpse as Xander passed. He had a startling number of dead animals in his wheelbarrow. Whatever had killed them had been busy.

"Awful thing. Dorvu won't touch them. He says they smell wrong."

Xander frowned at the small furry bodies.

"We're looking into it."

Horace nodded and moved to the bonfire where he disposed of the bodies. If the dragon said they smelt wrong, then dark magic was definitely involved. It was best to destroy them and thus the magic in case something more came of it.

Xander turned down the private path toward the professors' cottages and passed his own on the way to Mara's. The stream babbled to his left, a familiar and comforting sound. Green shoots peeked out at the edge of the bank. It seemed a little early, but given the proximity to Professor Hudson's cottage, he wasn't that surprised. The witch had an affinity for plants, and they tended to grow around her whether she intended it or not.

Something sent a chill down Xander's spine, and he paused to look around him. His magic came quickly, but he couldn't see anything in the darkness. The small breeze carried the scent of frost and wood fire, and the only sounds he heard were the small animals settling for the night. Shaking his head, he decided that he was paranoid and needed to stop procrastinating. This would be a difficult conversation, and he'd put it off all day.

He knocked on Mara's door and waited. Tucking his hands in his pockets away from the increasingly chilly air, Xander tried not to tap his foot. He'd never been very good at waiting, and that only increased around Mara. She finally opened the door in far more casual attire than what she wore around the students. Well-fitted jeans sat below a loose, elegant shirt that showed off the figure Xander had admired for decades now.

"We need to talk about the dead animals. I'm not behind it," Xander expressed bluntly, seeing no reason to beat around the bush.

Mara's hand tightened on the door, but she stepped aside to allow him into the cozy cottage. Well-worn bookshelves lined the walls of the short hallway, holding a mix of non-fiction relating to various magics and elf history and a few old fiction books. He removed his shoes and followed her into the living room. A pair of comfortable couches took up most of the floor space and faced a tall, open fireplace where a small fire crackled. The thin rug in front of the fireplace had long since lost its pattern and become nothing more than a soft blur on the bare wooden floor.

"I have not practiced dark magic in a long time," Xander stated.

"Not since we broke up, you mean."

"I did what was necessary. I couldn't sit by and see innocent people hurt."

"There were light magic options available to you."

"No, Mara. There weren't. You know damn well that they would have taken too long. We would never have won if we'd waited for those damn herbs and whatever else. Dark magic was the only way to save those people."

Mara closed her eyes and squeezed the bridge of her nose.

"And you're not behind the deaths of these animals?"

He took a step closer to her, wanting to soothe the tension in her shoulders. "No. I believe it's a Dark Mist. Someone performed a death spell. They must have."

"A Dark Mist like the one that hunted Leira?"

Xander looked away. "I believe so, yes."

Mara cursed under her breath.

"We need to be sure before we continue this. The students can't be told. Those who don't panic will try to take things into their own hands."

"You mean Alison Brownstone." Xander smiled.

"She follows her adopted parents very closely, but this isn't something she can be involved in." Mara shook her head, trying to quell the feeling of pride.

"We will deal with this quietly," he assured the headmistress.

"Are you sure it's the Dark Mist? Is there no other possibility?" Mara's eyes pleaded with him. "Nothing at all?"

"I'm not entirely sure yet, but I will be soon."

She slumped on the couch.

"I had hoped we were free of such things." She ran her thumb over the spine of the book she'd been reading. "I'd hoped that enough time had passed."

"As had I."

Jason sat up slowly and checked that his roommates were asleep before he slipped out of bed. It was past midnight, and the school was silent save for the quiet creaks of the wood settling in the cold air. He took a moment to initiate his stealth spell before he made his way to the professors' offices at a light-footed jog. Everyone was tucked safely in their beds, including the staff. He had the time and freedom he needed to enter Professor Heineken's office.

After a quick look around, he pulled his lock picks from the pocket of his pajamas and crouched to examine the lock. It had been magically adjusted to be more complicated than a standard office lock. Jason frowned. That only added to his suspicions. The professors weren't supposed to have anything dangerous in their offices. Why would Heineken have modified the lock if he wasn't hiding something?

Jason was increasingly sure that the professor was behind the dead animals on the grounds. He didn't know how or why, but there was something about the man that didn't sit right. Jason was something of an expert on hiding dark intentions, and he felt sure about his instincts on the matter.

The lock took far longer to pick than he wanted. He kept peering over his shoulder to make sure no one witnessed him breaking in. Finally, it unlocked with a soft snick, and Jason slipped inside. Locking it behind him when he finished would be the tricky part.

Rather than risk someone seeing a light orb, he pulled out his wand and cast a night vision spell. The office around him was quite standard. Floor to ceiling bookshelves covered the back wall, and a large pale-wood desk stood in front of them. Everything was neat and tidy, with a small pile of papers to the left of the writing space on the desktop. A slender silver pot held a variety of pens and a couple of pencils, but nothing stood out as suspicious.

Jason skimmed the leather spines of the books, looking for anything tied to dark magic. To his disappointment, most were about the mechanical workings of various vehicles and a couple on Oriceran history. He was ready to pick the small locks on the desk when a title on magical transfer and the art of alchemy caught his eye.

He pulled the book from the shelf and examined the pages for signs of having been bent or thumbed more than the others. No such luck. He flipped through and let the book fall open wherever the spine was slightly softer, indicating where it had been opened often. The chapter discussed the concept of storing magic in a variety of different vessels including crystals.

Jason put the book back and made quick work of the locks on the narrow desk drawers. Inside, he found a selection of delicate crystal vials, all empty. There were a small handful of engraved tumble stones, clear quartz, rose quartz, tiger's eye, and hematite. Jason hadn't taken the class on crystals and the magic related to them, so he didn't know what they were used for. The engravings were alien to him, too. He found a pen and pad and scribbled quickly so he could research them in the library.

A final look in the small filing cabinet revealed a spare set of clothes, more pens and notepads, and a list of mechanical-focused magic journals to recommend to his students. Jason sighed and left the office entirely dissatisfied. It took him almost fifteen minutes to re-lock the door. His thoughts about what he might have missed had been a severe distraction.

He was sure there was something to find and he wasn't ready to accept that the professor was innocent. Not yet.

Ira pulled the vial from the box beneath his bed. He was eager to begin his next experiment, but it required time and patience to set up correctly. The bright blue-white magic flickered and swirled within the small vial. That small quantity could change his world if he could bend it to his will and connect it to his own power. Therein lay the problem.

He had set aside the small office next to his bedroom as his ritual space. The furniture had been removed, leaving the room entirely bare and clean except for a clear circle of pure white candles that filled the center.

The professor placed the vial in a small silver dish in the middle of the circle and began exploring the magic he had obtained. He placed small crystals—simple tumble stones with individual engravings—between the candles. Moving clockwise in a slow, methodical fashion, he eased a thread of his magic into each crystal. Once the final stone rested between the last two candles, the magic came together to form a prism to contain his experiment.

A thrill of anticipation ran through him. He was sure that this kemana crystal was the one. Something about it called to him. He sat cross-legged in front of the silver dish and emptied his mind. There was no room for mistakes.

His magic rippled and surged into his hands, eager to taste the enchantment within the vial. When he succeeded, he would be unstoppable, and he would pave the way for his fellows. Slowly, he calmed himself and pushed his power back to avoid a reaction if the kemana crystal wouldn't sync with him. He tried again. The vial was icy cold to the touch, which Ira took as a good sign. The last one had felt like lava beneath his fingertips, and that had ended up in a catastrophic explosion. It had taken a large lump of his savings to pay off the right people to hide his connection to that.

Ira exhaled slowly and pulled the stopper carefully from the vial. The kemana crystal essence overflowed and crept out into the prism in delicate ribbons of pure blue-white. Ira remained perfectly still as the magic took the initiative and poked at the walls of its cage. He watched it carefully, looking for any signs of red or black, which would mean it wasn't compatible with his own magic.

He wished that he had Alison's vision so he could take a more scientific approach to everything. If he had such skill, he would be able to map out the threads within his magic and those of the crystal and align them. That was something he planned to do once the first transplant had been completed and he could go back to his brothers and show them it could be done. He would have far more resources, then. No more sneaking around.

The kemana crystal magic condensed and flowed back into the vial, having concluded it could not possibly return to its source. Ira smiled. The previous versions had fought until they sparked and damaged the surroundings. This was a very good sign indeed. He called his magic and pressed it tentatively against the opening of the vial and felt the crystal's essence push against it. He gasped, feeling like someone had driven a large blade into his lower back.

His magic retreated immediately, and he shoved the stopper back onto the flask. This wouldn't be quite as easy as he had initially hoped.

"This is my last chance." He frowned and placed the vial back in the dish. "This has to work."

CHAPTER EIGHT

L uke looked at the small group of freshmen and sophomores around him and smiled. Coach Regency had put each of them through their paces with magic and physical fitness. They'd all proven they could run, catch, and climb. Their magic needed work, but that was to be expected. What was left was the real potential.

He had one semester to train them into the team that would take them to the championships for the next couple of years. A quiet shifter who held back from the bustle of the main group had caught Luke's eye. He hadn't been flashy while proving his physical prowess, but he had easily surpassed the others in all the tests. He'd almost beaten Luke's scores. There was a determination below the surface, something that pleased his wolf. Maybe he was biased, but he would give him a shot regardless.

He nodded to the quiet student. "What's your name?"

The shifter lifted his eyes to look at Luke. "Matt."

"Any experience, Matt?"

A whisper rippled through the group about Luke giving preference to his own kind. Shifters were known for being excellent at sports, so it was only reasonable that they'd do well in Louper.

"Sure, some."

Luke looked around the group, assessing their body-language. He wanted confident, strong players who would take direction. A Light Elf and a pair of full-blooded wizards stood out. Their magic had been a little sloppy compared to some of the others, but they were eager to learn. They struck him as the type to work well as a team, whereas some of the others were too interested in showing off.

"You." He pointed to the elf and the wizards. "And you two." "Let's see what you can do with Matt." The other teammates stood on the sidelines, waiting their turns.

The wizards, both lean and fast with bright, sea-green eyes, grinned at him. The Light Elf wasn't as boisterous and simply walked over to the shifter.

"Clear some space." Luke waved the rest of the group from the field. "You have five minutes to run through the temple. I want to see your speed and ability to handle the magic."

Coach Regency had his usual glass of whiskey and allowed Luke to lead. The shifter had earned his place as team captain, and Max felt good about giving him free rein.

"Can we get the Aztec temple sim, coach?"

Max nodded and pulled up the setting. It was a small training ground intended to test skills rather than a full-blown game. Luke knew every inch of that temple and could run through it backward in the dark. It was versatile with several different magic types that could be added for extra difficulty. It would give him a good view of how the students worked together.

Matt and his three new teammates found themselves in the middle of a thick, humid jungle with large stone blocks seemingly growing from the dark ground. Unfamiliar birds called from the thick canopy overhead. The bright, pale winter sunlight had been replaced with an oppressive gloom.

"Four minutes, fifty-five seconds," Luke shouted.

Matt's ears pricked, and he heard the soft tick of a clock directly in front of them. He tried to listen past all the unfamiliar sounds from the birds and small creatures in the undergrowth and focused on anything that might be temple related.

"There's a narrow path there. He said it's the temple, so we need to head into the stone ruins," the Light Elf said.

Matt didn't argue. It was a reasonable bet. The tight time limit meant they couldn't be too far from their goal. The boys jogged along the narrow path between tall, broad-trunked trees and ducked under low-hanging vines. Matt swore a few of those hissed, but he ignored that in favor of watching his footing and looking out for the magic Luke had mentioned.

He held an arm out to stop the others when the ruins came into view. Tall, imposing stone walls extended to the dark, stormy sky in the middle of a clearing. The ground turned from dark earth to cracked and broken stone with small tufts of hardy greenery. The rugged edge of the rough pyramid-shaped temple loomed before them. Matt swore he could smell old blood, but he shrugged that off as his imagination. He'd done a lot of reading on the South American civilizations such as the Inca and their blood sacrifices.

"There." The dark-haired wizard pointed. "The magic."

They turned to see a trio of bright green orbs hovering over the dark abyss that formed the only visible entrance to the temple. Each looked about the size of a mango, and they flickered and emitted a soft buzzing sound. Matt's wolf wanted to stay far away from them. They looked as though they hurt.

"What type?" Matt looked at the wizard. "Any idea?"

The elf narrowed his eyes. "I believe it'll dive-bomb us and drop us out of the game."

No one argued. The elves were more closely tied to the magic, so it was likely that he did have a better grasp of its potential.

"So how do we get around it, or do we take it out?" Matt asked.

The blond wizard grinned. "We blind it. We envelope it in dark smoke so it can't see us."

"Do it." Matt stepped back to give them room to work.

The thick, warm air pressed against his back, and something sharp brushed his ankle. He remained still and focused on the wizards. Most small predators would leave him alone if he remained still and quiet. He would not lose this chance because he freaked out about a tarantula or something.

The wizards stopped at the edge of the clearing and

drew their slender wands. Matt noted the silver engraving within the pale wood and the expensive sneakers they wore. They were from money but had been nice enough so far at least. He still made a mental note about the money situation. Those from richer families often weren't all that pleasant to his kind. He'd been hurt enough in the past and had no intention of allowing that to happen again.

The blond wizard whispered under his breath and pointed his wand at the ground. Matt raised an eyebrow but let them proceed. The dark-haired wizard's expression turned to one of pained focus. A small, dark-red fire formed above the stone and the wizard crouched and blew on it as though extinguishing a candle.

Matt was impressed when the fire billowed into thick, dark smoke. The elf stepped forward and motioned slowly with his hands. The smoke surrounded the increasingly agitated orbs which had made no move toward either the fire or the students. Matt hoped that meant their field of view was limited to the courtyard and that their ploy would work.

"Run," the elf commanded.

They raced across the courtyard and dove into the darkness of the entryway. Matt's eyes adjusted quickly, revealing a tight tunnel with a low ceiling and smooth floor. A heavy buzzing followed by a sharp thud as the orbs struck the walls on either side of the entryway made Matt smile. They'd done it.

"Stay close to me." He walked confidently into the darkness. "I can see."

The others ran their hands along the walls on either side and waited patiently for their eyes to adjust. They hadn't learned any night-vision spells yet. Touching the walls was a risk, but it helped them navigate their surroundings better. Matt led them around a sharp left bend and revealed the gold token in a small room bathed in yellow light. The shifter grabbed the prize and grinned when the game faded away to reveal Luke clapping approval.

"Not bad." He looked at the group. "What are your names?"

The elf stared him down, challenging him. "Etienne. I transferred."

Luke allowed the aggression to slide despite his wolf wanting to remind the upstart of his place. He understood that it was difficult being a transfer student.

"Daniel." The dark-haired wizard pointed to the blond. "And Cody."

Luke pursed his lips. They clearly came as a pair, and that could be a problem. The team needed to work as one cohesive unit. Their bond would already be tighter than those of the team around them. Still, they had worked well in the temple.

Max saw the look of concern on Luke's face, but he had watched the other applicants closely.

The coach walked up to the students. "We'll keep them. Push them hard this week. Get them working like a well-oiled machine and we'll try them out in the next game."

Luke's jaw clenched. He understood that the gnome was the coach, but it still made him look weak in front of his new teammates.

"Understood, coach."

Luke turned to the rest of the applicants. "Better luck next time."

The wizards high-fived each other. Etienne smiled, and Matt allowed himself a momentary grin. They would need a lot of work, but it would give Luke something to focus on. The way his friends were acting and pushing him away stung. He needed something positive.

CHAPTER NINE

Alison took a sip of cool water and watched as Kathleen wriggled into her costume. This was the first costume fitting for the musical and hadn't gone entirely to plan. Kathleen frowned as the stage-hand helped her into the enormous underskirt that gave the feathery white skirt impressive volume. The bodice fit well, although Alison could already see the pale silver glitter coating Kathleen's arms. That would cover absolutely everything.

Kathleen lifted the top two layers of skirt and tried to peer at the floor.

"How am I supposed to walk?" She took a step forward, and her too-large heels tipped to the left. "Oh, this is hopeless. Can't I wear something more—"

"Tight? Revealing?" Alison couldn't keep the smirk off her face. "Galinda is supposed to be all pretty, floaty layers." She gestured at the dress.

Professor Fowler fixed Kathleen with a stern glare. "She's also supposed to be graceful and radiate confidence to the point of being the bad sister. She has a very high opinion of herself in *Wicked*."

Christie came up to Alison with a wide grin on her face as she clutched her long, green dress in her arms.

"Have you seen this? Oh, my word, isn't it the most beautiful thing?" She held the dress up so Alison could see more clearly. "I never thought I'd be able to wear green but it has stunning long arms with all this beautiful detailing. It's floor-length too. Not ideal with my height, but they've given me the prettiest black heels to wear with it. I thought the little emerald-green bows on the front were the most wonderful touch. I think I'll be fitted next. Have you seen your dress yet? Are you happy with it?"

Alison took a moment to process the rush of words.

"I haven't tried it on yet, but I have seen it." Alison held up the traditional black dress. "I'm quite fond of it."

"Oh, that is lovely. How do you feel about being a half-Drow playing the wicked witch? I mean, it's quite fitting, isn't it? Oh, I'm so sorry, that was horribly rude of me. You have to admit there is a link there, though, not that you don't have the most beautiful voice."

Alison smiled. "I do think there's something poetic about my playing the role of Elphaba. I've thought about my place in the world lately. There's something a little cathartic about playing the role, I think. Someone who's basically good but really misunderstood." Alison picked up the traditional black witch's hat. "And it's fun playing with the stereotypes and turning them on their head. I know a little of what that's like."

Kathleen pranced down the center of the room where everyone tried to get dressed and talk to the costume designers about adjustments. Someone had supplied her with shoes that fit, and she made the most of it.

"Doesn't she look beautiful? The movement in the skirt is gorgeous. It looks like it's alive in a really nice way. I mean, it flows like water, but it has that feathery layer on top that makes it interesting. The bodice isn't overdone, and it would have been so easy to add too much glitter and sparkle, but I think they did a beautiful job." Christie admired Kathleen. "She helped with the design, didn't she?"

Kathleen beamed and ran her hands over the skirt. "Yes, I did, and it's almost there. It needs a finishing touch."

Alison smiled at her friend. She had really found her calling.

The costume designer in charge of the outfit ushered her away to fuss over her again.

An older witch touched Christie's elbow. "Come along. Let's see how this fits. I suspect those sleeves will be a little too long."

Alison put the witch's hat on and smiled at herself in the mirror. It looked absolutely absurd, and she loved that. Holding the black dress up in front of her, she enjoyed the moment. The black garment hung to the floor and had a high neckline with full-length sleeves. Delicate lace detailing added a little interest over the hips and to the neckline, but it was simple—something that Alison appreciated. The dress allowed her performance to speak for herself while also being a key part of the character.

The areas in front of the mirrors and behind the curtains were taken. Christie emerged not long after Alison wondered if she should find a space to try the dress on.

The younger girl had been entirely transformed. Her hair was pinned loosely on top of her head, and the fitted green dress was stunning. The tips of the long sleeves fell to her knees when her arms hung at her sides, and the neckline was lower than anything Alison had seen her in before. The glowing happiness within her energy said everything, though. Christie had been a new person since the incident with the pendant.

"What do you think?" Christie chewed her bottom lip. "Does it look ridiculous?"

"It looks as though you were made for this role," Alison said.

Luke rolled his shoulders and ignored the light rain, a fine mist that would chill them without soaking them. The new Louper players were in sweats and t-shirts, ready for their first official training session.

"Physical fitness is as important as magic." He waited for the team to comment. "We need to be able to out-run, out-climb, and generally be better, faster, and stronger than our opponents. Today, we'll go over the assault course."

Matt's eyes brightened a touch at that. It was something the shifters would be better at, which made it easier for Luke to lead them through. He struggled a little to understand and focus on the magic portion of training. Coach Regency had made himself comfortable on a large canvas seat, complete with his usual glass of whiskey. Luke looked pointedly at him, and the coach snapped himself out of his thoughts and formed the assault course for them.

Daniel, the dark-haired wizard, gasped when he saw the towering nets, deep pits of dark murky water, and tall wooden constructions.

"We'll do three full circuits of this course. The time to beat is four minutes and ten seconds." Luke looked meaningfully at them. His wolf itched to get started.

The coach held up a stopwatch. "Three. Two. One. Go!"

Matt was side-by-side with Luke when they raced up the short dirt path to the first obstacle—a large net they needed to climb and throw themselves over the top. It was almost two stories high and would take strength and endurance. Luke remembered the cliffs he'd had to climb in a grueling match the previous year and knew that pushing the new Louper players through this was the right thing to do.

Etienne wasn't far behind the shifters. He launched himself at the net and climbed up with as much speed and determination as he could muster. He had a point to prove. He'd come into the year halfway through the previous semester and as such, hadn't formed a solid friendship group like the others. As far as his classmates were concerned, he was the foreign elf with the odd accent.

Daniel and Cody climbed side-by-side, pushing each other on with small looks and a familiarity that came from years spent together. They'd grown up next door and had been inseparable since they were toddlers. Nothing would change that.

Luke threw himself over the log at the top of the net and began the quick descent.

"Get a move on." He dropped the last few feet. "Clock's ticking!"

Next came a balance test. A series of three logs stretched above an almost black pit of water. The logs had a metal rod through the middle which made them spin the moment you stepped on them. Luke knew he needed to be fast and well-balanced to make it across without being dunked. Trying to do the rest of the course while dripping wet was absolutely miserable.

Matt hopped onto the first log. His eyes went wide as it twisted beneath his feet. His arms windmilled, but he recovered and hurried to the second one. Etienne, having seen what would happen if he wasn't careful, almost danced across the center of the log. His nimble movements had earned him insults from other students, but they were a benefit in challenges like that. He was right behind the shifters when they reached the monkey bars.

Etienne noted that Matt had already begun to tire. He needed to improve his endurance, something the elf didn't lack. He overtook the shifter on the bars and dove under the low net at the same moment Luke did. The wizards scowled at being left behind and pushed themselves harder, keeping up with Matt now. Etienne crawled through the mud beneath the net, keeping his eyes front and center. Luke was his captain, but he would still do everything in his power to win this.

The other three remained side-by-side and a camaraderie grew between them.

"Is this course growing?" Daniel panted as he gripped the rope. "I'm pretty sure it's gotten longer."

He pushed off the wooden platform and swung across

the black pit below. He barely managed to land on the plat-form on the other side. Matt grabbed his shirt and pulled him up.

"I wouldn't be surprised. And we have to do two more laps after this." Cody looked back at how much they'd already done. "I don't think I'll survive."

Etienne and Luke were an obstacle ahead of the others now. While Matt and the wizards scrambled over a series of increasingly taller walls, they made their way through the log jumps. Luke admired the way Etienne flowed like water under the tall logs and over the short ones. It had taken the shifter months to find a rhythm across this part of the course, especially when fatigue kicked in.

Daniel paused and looked at the rows of logs in front of them. He placed his hands on his hips and groaned.

"Think of the championships. Visualize that trophy." Cody patted him on the back.

Matt now had his second wind, but he reminded himself that they needed to do two more circuits. It was better to hang back and form a team bond.

Luke glanced at his watch. There was a small chance that Etienne might be able to beat the previous record set by Henry. The final obstacle was a heap of old car tires scattered about at all angles, leaving no way to find a rhythm or pattern. You had no choice but to scramble and try to keep your balance as your foot slipped on the wet rubber.

Etienne steadied his breathing and jumped onto the first tire. He seemed to hop from foothold to foothold, and Luke watched in awe and wondered if the elf had cat in him somewhere. Henry would be very upset to hear his record had been beaten by an elf.

———

Peter looked at the plans for the big senior project for Entrepreneurs Club. They had found a way to mix magic with techno music to make the music change based on the mood of the people in the room. That meant clubbers and dancers would always have the very best experience. It was tricky to pull off, but the group was confident they could manage it.

He was particularly excited that he could write about it in his Journalism Club and the school newspaper, too, giving him extra credit. He could see the front-page spread already.

"We need to start simple with a few bars of dubstep since it's less complicated than hardcore or electronica." Ella pointed at the sheets of music spread before them. "There's too much risk if we dive in with a full, complicated song."

"What about our ROI?" Adam looked at the small group. "Do we have buyers lined up for this?"

They planned to use the profits from the invention to help pay their college fees.

"There are a few clubs in Richmond." Ella pulled out the list of potential buyers. "It's a bit of a drive, but they'll pay better rates than the locals."

Peter rolled a small silver tube in his palm. "We also need to calculate the transportation. The tubes don't look nice enough for the price we're asking."

"Don't forget we need to pin down exactly how much to sell at once. No one will buy it by the hour, so we must decide how long a reasonable night is," Ella reminded them, pushing the music aside in favor of charts.

"And safeguard it from thieves." Adam tidied the papers. "We don't want people taking the idea and undercutting us."

"I thought we'd found out the right locking mechanism? Did the Celtic knot spell not hold up?" Peter frowned.

Sarah stretched her legs out under the table. "The money didn't work out. We'd have to switch over to copper, and the margins don't look very good."

Peter ran his fingers through his hair. The copper issue was one they continually ran into, and it frustrated him. Copper was an excellent magical conductor, but it was also expensive. They had no luck with aluminum, and iron was too prone to corruption. Wood was a no-go, as the way it handled magic wasn't feasible.

"What about bronze? How do those margins look?" Peter studied the chart. "Hmm, still not enough. Could we work with crystals? Or glass?"

Ella picked up a glass stone. "No. It's too difficult to find ones that won't alter the delicate notes of music." She rummaged through the papers. "Here. You can see that while crystals are great for sturdier spells, they crush the musical notes which makes them sound flat."

Peter slumped in the seat. This was their big project. They had to find a way around the problem. It had seemed like such a good idea when they'd come up with it, but they'd found more problems than solutions.

"We need something that looks cool and that the

humans will be okay with." Peter looked around for inspiration. "What about a USB stick or something?"

Ella sighed. "Too plain. We need this to be flashy, so the humans can show it off as a status symbol. That's our big advantage here."

Cody leaned forward. "Why don't we double it up with something else? I mean, we're working on those butterflies, right?"

"You think the magic would run down the copper wires? How much copper would we need? Could the margins be good enough?" Adam pulled up the price charts.

Peter grinned. "The humans would be really impressed. Magically-fueled butterflies that play music to their tastes? I think we're onto something."

"The margins look good. We need to figure out how to combine the magic that brings the butterflies to life with the music, though." Adam retrieved the music sheets. "I think it could be done."

Peter jumped up, excited. "It'll be finicky and delicate, but we can thread the life down the center of the butterfly and have the music in the wings. We can add silk to the wings for color, and the organic matter would help refine and hone the music."

A small cheer went around the room. They had finally made real progress. Now, the hard work could begin.

Jason gazed at the board at the front of the classroom and wondered if maybe he should have quit Foreign Language

Club. He'd joined it because his parents insisted. Learning foreign languages and cultures would make traveling the world and infiltrating organizations and social circles easier. He was already fluent in Spanish, German, and Russian, and he was almost there with French. Magic helped them learn quicker, of course. The spells flowed as easily as fresh spring rain when they had been cast so frequently. The words were inserted into the student's mind, and the spell's design opened the mind and allowed it to become more sponge-like. It had started as a minor study aid, but the students had adapted and perfected it.

The Entrepreneurs Club would love to get their hands on that charm if they knew it existed, Jason thought to himself. He plastered a polite smile on his face and waited for the spell's peculiar sensation to wash over him. It felt like he'd left his body ever so slightly, creating more room and pliability for the knowledge. His mind wandered to the dead animals and Professor Heineken. He'd tried to change classes so he could study the man in person and have a better chance of seeing him slip up. Unfortunately, given that there was only one semester left, there was no chance of that.

Jason allowed the professor's words to pass through him rather than paying any real attention. The spell meant that the lesson on French culture would remain once the club was over for the afternoon. A darkness passed the doorway, and Jason frowned. It hadn't seemed corporeal, but that was impossible. There was too much magic in the school, and the defenses against any and all forms of dark magic were stringent.

He replayed the glimpse of the darkness over and over

in his mind. Could he have been wrong about Professor Heineken? Or was he into something far darker than Jason had initially thought? He had assumed the professor was dabbling in something to extend his life a little, something ashy grey on the scale of dark magic. It wasn't what you'd call entirely ethical, but it wouldn't get anyone killed.

Jason needed to get into Professor Heineken's cottage, but students weren't allowed anywhere near the professors' residences, and the man would likely be there once classes ended. He hadn't seen a schedule of his teaching times and office hours, but Jason was sure he could secure one from somewhere. He made a mental note to track his target's usual patterns, too. If Professor Heineken was dabbling in something dark enough to sneak through the school defenses, he needed to be stopped.

CHAPTER TEN

Alison was restless. Her roommates' souls were the peaceful pale-blues of sleep, but she needed to wander the grounds. She retrieved the small telescope Izzie had given her and smiled as she felt the soft wisp of magic on it. When she closed her eyes, she could share the peace and contentment Izzie felt at that moment.

She wrapped herself in her warm coat and boots and headed outside. It was her last semester at the school, and it was a time of change. She wanted to speak to Horace and Dorvu. The telescope in hand, Alison set out across the frosty grass toward a small knoll where she could sit. The sky was bright and clear, showing the sprinkling of stars overhead. A smile spread across her face as she felt Izzie's happiness deepen. It was like she was right there right beside her.

Dorvu cavorted between the trees as Alison settled on the grass and lifted the telescope to her eye. Wherever Izzie was, they looked at the same set of stars that night.

There was comfort in that knowledge. The dark mist that had emerged from the pendant had rattled her a little. It wasn't so much the mist itself but the fact she hadn't told her friends yet. She hated keeping things from them, and she knew that the longer she waited, the worse it would be. Still, there hadn't been an appropriate time.

A puff of frosty white breath formed on the edge of the trees and a squeal followed quickly. The dragon snapped his jaws shut around something round and feathered. "Best not get struck by Dorvu's ice-breath," Alison said to herself.

The creature wove in and out of the trees in search of his next snack. The plump bird hadn't satisfied his hunger, but everything roosted at that time of night. Giving up for the evening, he landed near Horace in his usual spot by the fire near the barn. The flames sent shadows skittering across the wooden wall and cast Dorvu as far bigger and more menacing than he was. He circled a few times and settled on the bare earth with a petulant expression on his face.

Alison approached the gamekeeper and the dragon with a smile, her telescope safely tucked away inside her coat.

"What's wrong, Dorvu?"

The dragon looked at her and huffed, almost putting the fire out.

"My food is dwindling. Whatever is killing the animals makes it difficult to hunt. The animals are more cautious and harder to find."

Alison frowned and saw the latest small pile of furry bodies Horace was disposing of.

"I don't know what's causing it. There's no blood and no injury that I can see." The gamekeeper dropped a few more corpses on the fire. "Don't you worry yourself, though. Professor Powell is looking into it."

Alison pursed her lips. The professor had experience with dark magic, everyone knew that, but it didn't mean he had the full story. She might have to speak to him privately and tell what happened in the woods with the rogue shifter.

"Something on your mind?"

Horace drew her from her thoughts, and she smiled.

"I'm wondering what could have killed them."

"You leave that to Professor Powell. You've heard from Izzie?"

"She gave me a telescope and left me a note. She's having a good time and considers it all a big adventure."

Horace nodded and smiled.

"You'll be applying for colleges soon."

"I'm planning to major in criminal psychology and minor in musical theatre."

"That's good. You should do what you're passionate about. The world needs some more music and light."

Something felt wrong. Alison felt the slight drop in temperature before she saw the shift in magic. The enchanted lights around the school buildings flickered and dimmed to almost nothing before they flared to their full shine.

She peered at them, trying to see a mystical trail or fingerprint that would reveal exactly what had happened or at least caused it. It was as though something had tugged the magic away from the lights for a moment, but she found nothing.

"I've never seen that before. I think it's time you went back inside," Horace advised with a quick look at the building.

Alison bristled at the groundskeeper's words, but he wasn't entirely wrong. She was, after all, alone, and while she was confident with her magic, there was no point to unnecessary risks. If something could take the essence from the lights, what was to say it couldn't take hers as well?

She walked slowly across the grass and paused to inspect each of the magical lights above her. Their slender stems appeared to be intact, and she couldn't detect any signs of tampering. Each shone a brilliant silvery-white with no cracks or shimmers of other colors. She made a mental note to look in the library for beings and spells that could drain magic like that.

Ira was finally ready to attempt moving the kemana crystal's magic into himself. He had ordered rare herbs and sand from the middle east. They had arrived that morning, and he had devoted all evening to his preparations. The magic remained in the vial, but he hadn't missed the way it had dulled while away from the main crystal. Still, if he could take this step, he would be closer to draining the main crystal directly.

The professor told himself that this wasn't dark magic

or even unethical. If he could find a way to transplant magic from a large store into a person, the potential was huge. He could help strengthen warriors, heal people whose magic had been damaged, and far more. His study had been transformed into a truly magical space. Ira had painstakingly painted the necessary symbols on the walls in silver and navy-blue paint. Each one had taken an age as he'd measured and re-measured to make sure it was placed precisely and each angle on the symbol was perfect. The vial remained safely in the silver bowl in the middle of the room, waiting for him.

Ira rubbed the scar on his hand from the time he had tried to draw the magic directly from a crystal into himself. He had learned so much since then. If only his fellows could see him now, they would understand that he wasn't some weak younger man to be shunned. He would transform the world around them.

The herbs were pungent and had been difficult to hide. He'd had them shipped into Charlottesville rather than to the school directly, trying to avoid too many questions. The contact he had in the town had increased the fee for receiving the delivery, and his savings were dwindling. He needed this to work.

Each herb had been carefully ground and mixed in a copper bowl to which Ira now added spring water and three drops of his own blood. From a young age, he had been told that anything to do with blood magic was evil and not to be touched. How closed-minded those people were. He dipped a slender paintbrush into the paste formed by the herbs and began painting the swirling symbols on the floor outside the circle of candles and crystals. The herbs and symbols would focus the magic and draw it through into his hands.

He hadn't been able to check if his magic was compatible, but time was ticking, and he needed to make real progress. Sometimes, risks were necessary. The final symbol was particularly complicated with intersecting circles and spirals that had to be spaced carefully so the meaning and purpose didn't accidentally change.

Ira stepped into the circle and slowed his breathing, then lit the candles, starting from the southernmost point. He whispered the incantation he had found in a book hidden centuries before in a Mayan temple. It must have come from Oriceran originally. The thick guttural language felt as though it stuck to his tongue and made his lips numb, but he persevered until the final candle was lit.

The magic within the small vial sparked and thrashed, reacting to the tug from the power imbued in the symbols and ritual work around Ira. He knelt in front of the silver dish and slowly removed the stopper.

Rather than the magic curling around his fingers and joining with his magic, it shot out to the closest hematite crystal, turning it a vivid blood-red. To Ira's horror, every light around the school grounds dimmed to almost darkness as their magic flooded his ritual circle. The candles went out, and the crystals rattled and skittered along the wooden floor. The herbs fluttered upward and formed small tornadoes of greens and oranges in the soft starlight filtering in through the window.

The power from the lights battered Ira's protective prism and his own mental defenses. It was all over in a matter of seconds, and he fell onto his side, gasping for breath as sweat dripped from his brow and his hands shook. He felt like he had fought an entire army. Every muscle ached, and his joints protested. His nerves felt as though they caught fire and he lost consciousness.

CHAPTER ELEVEN

Professor Fowler stood in her kitchen watching a pot of water come slowly to a rolling boil. She smiled and breathed in the rich scent of dried herbs filling the room. Her window sills were packed with plants of various shapes and sizes, and more hung from the corners of the ceiling. Long tendrils of thin, vine-like stems draped in front of the side window, bearing tiny white flowers which gave off a faint sweet smell.

The day had gone quite well, but she was ready to curl up with a good book and relax for the evening. She'd picked up something by her favorite author a couple of days ago and had looked forward to slipping between the pages all day. The water reached full boil, and she moved it from the flame to cool before she added the black tea with small dried blue flowers to her teapot. She scooped half a teaspoon of locally sourced honey into her plant-themed mug and poured the water.

She carried the tray into her comfortable living room where a long, deep-green couch was the centerpiece. The night had drawn in and the bright lights around the school grounds shone gently through the trees, adding a pale, white cast to her room. She placed the tray down on the well-worn wooden table in front of the couch and pulled a handmade blanket around her before she picked up the paperback.

Peace and serenity filled her home, which always washed away any tension she might have gained through the day. Slowly, she lost herself in the latest adventures of the elven warrior on Oriceran. The tea was almost over-steeped when she reached the end of the second chapter. Professor Fowler had just poured when the lights on the grounds dimmed to almost nothing before returning.

Frowning, she slipped on her comfortable shoes and went out into her back garden to investigate. The small square of land was entirely hers with a neat wooden fence around the perimeter. It served to keep her plants from growing into the surrounding area rather than to keep others out. Herbs, flowers, and shrubs filled nearly every space.

Professor Fowler looked into the semi-darkness, listening for anything odd. The soft babbling of the stream was the only thing she heard. She assumed it was a small glitch somewhere and turned to go back inside when she saw a small songbird dead in the middle of the narrow path to her back gate. Professor Fowler approached the small feathered body slowly. Its bright red feathers were slightly dulled, and its beady eyes stared accusingly into the darkness. She reached down and picked it up gently. The body was already cold, and there were no signs of attack.

She frowned. "Dorvu didn't do this. There are no frost marks, and he eats what he kills."

A chill ran through her as she peered into the darkness which suddenly seemed far deeper. A sensation of being watched overtook her. She pulled her cardigan tighter and placed the bird beneath a bush. Horace could deal with it in the morning.

With one final look at the darkness, she returned to the warmth and safety of her cottage. For the first time since she'd moved there, she locked the door and closed the curtains, wanting to shut out the world beyond those walls.

Jason slipped out of bed once more. Having found nothing of real use in Professor Heineken's office, he planned to try to access the professors' private library. Rumor had it that there were many forbidden books locked away behind that door. If Jason wanted to find out what was going on, he needed more information.

Once again, he formed his stealth spell and set out along the corridors. Rather than heading left toward the offices, he turned right into the truly private area dedicated to the professors' lounge and library. He pulled his lock-picks and knelt before the imposing black door.

A clear gold plaque marked the room as being the private library. Even the gnomes had to get permission to step foot in there, or so the stories went. Jason had been able to access rare and dangerous books on dark magic thanks to his contacts, but this school had connections even his family didn't.

A quiet voice in the back of his mind said that his family would be proud of him and bring him back into the fold if he could take a few of those books. There was sure to be something of great value to them in there. Jason gritted his teeth. He wasn't walking that path anymore. He no longer wanted to feel their embrace.

"This is the second time I have found you trying to break into somewhere you shouldn't be, Mr. Parker."

Jason spun and feigned innocence as he faced Professor Powell.

He cursed under his breath and tried to hide the lock-picks, but the man's eyes tracked the movement.

"Give them here. Now." The professor held out his hand.

Jason relinquished them and searched for a suitable lie. He couldn't say that it was for a class. The professors would never set an assignment like that. A bet or dare was out, too— he'd look like a weak-willed fool, and no one would believe that.

"Well. What are you doing?"

Jason lifted his chin and attempted his most charming smile.

"I've heard all sorts of interesting rumors about what's in that library, and I wanted to see for myself."

Professor Powell raised his eyebrow. The words sounded truthful, and that was entirely unexpected.

"Did you plan to steal some of those books?"

Jason paused and thought for a moment. If he said yes, the consequences could be severe, but would the man believe him if he said no?

"No. I wanted to satisfy my curiosity."

The professor took a step closer. Typically, he wouldn't be in the school building at that time of night, but he'd been absorbed in his own studies and hadn't noticed time slipping by. Jason was clearly up to something, but what? The connection between Ira's office and the private library was an easy one to make. He had noticed something odd about Ira himself.

"If you are caught wandering around where you shouldn't be one more time, you will spend every evening for the rest of the school year in detention."

Jason nodded and turned to head back to his bed.

"Do you understand, Mr. Parker?"

"Yes, sir."

Professor Powell let him pass and watched him walk toward the dorms. Once Jason was out of sight, he whispered the password and enchantment that had been chosen for the semester and walked into the private library.

There were a few dangerous books on the dark-wood shelves, some of which he had donated from his own collection as a way of proving that he had left that part of his life behind. Xander ran his fingertips over the spells around the bookshelves and was satisfied that no one had touched them in a few days. Jason hadn't managed to get inside. He would have to keep a closer eye on him.

CHAPTER TWELVE

L uke shook his arms to release his nerves. This was his first Louper game of the season, and he had almost a brand-new team around him. A few of the veteran players had to quit to focus on grades and getting into college. No college was giving out Louper scholarships.

That left him with only a couple of players who were tested on the field. His new teammates had shown a lot of determination and potential in training and he hoped that was enough.

Matt stretched slowly and tried to ignore the crowd gathering in the stands. This was the first game of the season, and if they won, they would keep building toward the championship games. There was a lot of pressure for his first game to see how well he could lead the new team. Etienne smiled and patted him softly on the back. "We have a good captain." He looked at Luke. "He'll guide us well."

The elf had relaxed over the course of the week, and

Matt had started to like him. He'd come across as stuck-up and defensive at first, but the shifter could understand that. It was hard entering an established social group.

"Ready?" Luke looked at each of his teammates in turn. "We'll kick ass."

They gave a small cheer and tried to look more confident than they felt as they walked onto the field. Coach Regency was on the sidelines with an extra-large glass of whiskey. He smiled stiffly. This was a big risk with new season just underway and elimination with just one loss. The new players had a lot of potential, but it was down to Luke to pull them together for success.

The crowd quieted as the team descended into the virtual world of the match. Cody groaned when the air became thick and wet with humidity and the now familiar scent of jungle filled his nostrils. Mosquitoes buzzed, and small poisonous frogs croaked from the trees packed closely around them.

Luke feigned relief. "This makes our lives easier. It'll be like we practiced. We aim for the temple."

It wasn't easier at all. Yes, they had practiced in their own temple set-up, but the jungles were some of the more brutal terrains available to them. His team still needed to build their stamina, which could hinder them greatly.

Luke and Matt sniffed the air for the scent of stone and dry earth that often indicated the temples.

"That way." Luke pointed. "Come on. The other team will be moving already."

Matt remained close and Etienne brought up the rear with the aim of protecting their backs should they need it.

The wizards, Daniel and Cody, moved with far more confidence through the tight boughs and uneven terrain than they had in their first trial. They still lacked the certainty and balance of the others, though. Etienne grabbed Cody's shirt and stopped him from tripping over a thick vine. The wizard smiled and jogged to catch up with the shifters.

Alison leaned against Tanner when the rival team emerged into a large clearing. They were a good ten minutes ahead of the Cardinals already. The opposing team paced slowly along the tree line, trying to assess the situation. Three huge pyramids towered over them in a neat triangle. Each was well-worn with tall layers that would be difficult to climb with any speed.

"Come on, guys, you can do this. Remember, even breathing and don't exhaust yourself too early. You've improved by leaps and bounds since the tryouts," Luke encouraged, helping the wizards over a small stream.

The trees began to thin around them. The thick layer of leaves hiding poisonous bugs and snakes shrank away, revealing pale dirt. Luke stopped within the trees and looked at the pyramids before them. Each stretched toward the sky, a carefully carved mass of pale yellowish and grey stone. Small, pitch-black entrances were visible on the bottom layer and near the very top.

Cody leaned against a tree and studied the nearest pyramid. "I don't see any magic. Maybe the difficulty's inside?"

"No, I can feel something. Something dark." Etienne frowned.

A scream cut through the air, and Luke saw one of the

rivals race across the courtyard and into the trees with a trio of skeletal warriors with sharp spears chasing her.

Two more warriors ran from between the pyramids. They stopped in the center of the courtyard, their jaguar pelts draped over muscular backs. Cody's eyes went wide when he saw the jaguar skulls on their heads with brightly colored feathers sewn into the back to form a strange crest. Their chests were bare and painted with what looked suspiciously like blood. A white skirt-like garment of pale hide covered their hips and hung to their knees, but it was the vicious swords they held that caught the wizard's attention.

Cody swallowed. "So, we have living warriors and skeletal warriors. How do we deal with them?"

"Battle magic." Luke grinned at him. "You guys have studied that, right?"

"Yea." Cody shrugged and pushed off the tree. "Absolutely."

Daniel didn't look nearly so nonchalant, but Etienne had a large, feral grin on his face. His family had a proud line of guardians and protectors, and he'd been taught battle magic from a young age.

The elf stepped forward. "Use your fire magic and focus on their feet. We can handle the rest."

The elf formed a pair of deep-blue swords from thin air, his eyes never leaving the warriors. He'd trained for something like this for years, and it was time to prove his worth to the team.

The wizards' expressions turned to one of deep focus as they pulled their wands and worked together to form small fires around the enemy's feet. The warriors screamed, a sound of unadulterated rage.

"On three, we run to the far pyramid." Etienne looked at Luke for confirmation. "If Daniel and Cody can keep the fires going to slow them, we can take them down."

Matt and Luke allowed their wolves forward to take advantage of the strength and speed that would give them. The wizards worked hard to hide their fear.

"We haven't tried weaving fire spells on the move. What if we screw up?" Daniel swallowed.

Then we'll figure it out. Luke took a step forward. The glint of gold on the farthest pyramid caught his eye. *Run fast.* Only Matt could hear his commands while he was in wolf form. He was going to have to show the others what he wanted them to do.

He exploded out of the trees with Matt close behind. Etienne held back a little to protect the wizards. To Cody's alarm, a small army of warriors—skeletal and human-like—rushed out of all three structures.

The team raced forward, ducking and weaving around flying spears and slashing swords. The shifters drove the warriors to the ground while Etienne cut them down with his blades. The wizards remained close together. Sweat ran down their brows as they tried to avoid the attacks while maintaining the fires at their targets' feet.

They were all gulping air when Luke launched himself up the first step of the third pyramid. They could see the gold disk at the top, but they weren't the only ones. Members of the rival team skidded around the left pyramid and threw themselves onto the steps. Everyone pushed hard to climb the tall layers as quickly as they could, trying to ignore their absolute exhaustion.

Thick, dark-green vines emerged from small cracks between the great blocks. Daniel groaned, but Etienne sliced them away and scrambled up the levels. Cody and Daniel burned all the greenery they saw, but they found it increasingly difficult to access their magic.

Luke turned to look at them. He really needed to improve their stamina.

Matt was right at his side with a determined glint in his eye. By some miracle, they were one and a half layers above the rivals. They would pull this off.

The spectators watched with bated breath as the Cardinals slowed with each layer, pulling each other up in their determination to reach the gold disk. Thick storm clouds bubbled and pelted the team with big, heavy raindrops. The water streamed down the pyramid, making it slippery and difficult to get a good grip. Luke and Matt hauled the others up and pushed them on. They were a team.

Luke knew it was important that they did this as a squad. They needed those bonds. Seeing Luke racing ahead to get the disk wouldn't help morale.

"One more step," he called.

They each took a deep breath and reached for the lip of the final layer. The wizards dug deep and found a small well of energy to draw on as their muscles grew shaky and weak. They all made it to the final level of the pyramid, and Luke stepped aside to let Cody and Daniel jointly take the disk. They lifted it high above their heads and the match ended, returning them to the field and a standing ovation from the crowds around them.

Matt put his arm around Etienne's shoulders. "Dude, you were amazing."

The elf grinned. "It was all the captain."

Everyone patted Luke on the back and thanked him for keeping them going. The shifter couldn't keep the huge grin off his face. He was so proud of his new team. It had been a brutal landscape, but they'd pulled it off. They were one step closer to the championship.

CHAPTER THIRTEEN

I t was April Fool's day, and Ethan had spent months preparing for that morning. He had researched and refined his magic so that he could pull off something memorable. It was his last one at the school after all.

He ran his thumb over his focus bands and whispered the final words. Opening his eyes, he looked around. Everything seemed normal. Frowning, he walked to the closest door and opened it. Instead of a normal classroom, it was the dining hall. He restrained a whoop of joy and jogged back to his dorm room. Everyone would know it was him, but that didn't mean he wanted to get caught.

When he opened the door, he found himself looking at the headmistress's office. He swore under his breath. He hadn't thought this through quite as well as he believed he had.

"You're up early." Luke stood in his blue-striped pajamas and studied him curiously.

"I was just—"

"Setting up your yearly prank. I figured as much." He

smirked. Ethan closed the door to hide what lay behind it and Luke narrowed his eyes.

"What have you done this time?"

Ethan folded his arms and didn't say a word. He wanted people to see for themselves. Luke touched the doorknob cautiously with his fingertips. When it didn't electrocute him, he twisted it and opened the door, only to find himself looking at the potions' lab.

"Every door?"

Ethan couldn't restrain himself any longer.

"Every single door in the main school building." He grinned like a Cheshire cat.

Luke groaned and leaned against the wall.

"Including the bathrooms?"

"I'm not a monster."

The shifter squeezed the bridge of his nose.

"And how am I supposed to find our room and get changed into my uniform for the day?"

Ethan looked at his own pajamas. He didn't want the entire school to see them.

"I hadn't thought about that part—"

"Of course you didn't."

Alison removed her glasses and looked closely at her dorm room door. Neon-green and violent-pink threads of magic formed a weird web-type pattern across it. They hadn't been there when she went to sleep.

"Watch out for Ethan's pranks." Kathleen nudged her. "He'll aim big this year."

"I think he's already set it up. There's some weird magic on the door." Alison took a step closer to the entry.

"There's no way Ethan can magic an entire door," Kathleen scoffed.

"He has far more talent than you give him credit for, especially now that he has those focusing bands," Aya announced, tying her hair back.

The girls headed down to the dining hall in search of breakfast. Alison noticed that every door they passed had a similar web of magic. She wasn't sure what it meant but knowing Ethan, it would somehow lead to chaos.

They opened the large double doors to the dining hall and found themselves looking at a very confused Professor Hudson sitting behind her desk.

"Can I help you, girls?"

"This was supposed to be the dining hall…" Alison ran her finger over a thread of magic, "I believe Ethan has outdone himself this year."

Professor Hudson stood and walked around her desk. "Ethan did what? Transported you?"

"In a way. I believe he's switched the doors around, which is quite a feat." Alison smiled.

"Ah, so it's Ethan who wreaked havoc on the school this morning." The headmistress stood behind them with her arms folded. "Do you know where he is?"

"No idea."

"His room?"

"Not a clue," the girls all said at once.

Alison closed the dining hall door and re-opened it to find their dorm room. She peered at the magic to see exactly how it worked. She couldn't see any illusion spells, so it was likely that the doors did actually change the location to where they opened.

"You have to admit, it's a masterpiece." Ethan grinned and walked up to them.

"What are you wearing?" Kathleen gestured at his pajamas. "Where's your uniform?"

Ethan blushed. "I finished the spell before I got changed, and now, I can't find my room."

The headmistress leveled a glare at him.

"You will tell me exactly what you did right this second and then you will undo it."

Confused cries began to fill the hallways as people discovered the prank. Some were lucky, but mostly, people were bewildered and grew increasingly angry.

"Well... I found an old transportation spell. They used it on apples and things. I added that to a portal spell and finished it with something like a random number generator, so the place each opens to will be random." He looked very pleased himself. "It's a work of genius."

Mara's mouth thinned into a tight white line.

"I will admit that it is rather clever. However, the school cannot function like this."

Alison looked at the web to find the random number generator magic. Perhaps if she could identify that, she could tweak it to open the door to the correct location.

Ethan drew his wand and whispered some words. The web on the door shivered and turned bright purple before it pulsed and shimmered in shades of lilac and daffodil-yellow. Alison opened the door cautiously and found it now led onto the middle of a field.

Headmistress Berens clenched her jaw and breathed

slowly. She had looked forward to a peaceful cup of tea with her fellow professors before the school day started.

"You don't know how to undo this do you?" She turned to Ethan.

He chewed on his bottom lip. "I thought I did..."

The headmistress sighed. "Alison, can you see anything that might help us remove this spell? Anything at all?"

"A dissolution spell will cover it." Professor Powell jogged down the hallway. "The magic isn't firmly attached to the door so it won't harm anything other than the spell itself."

Ms. Berens nodded and rubbed her temples. She was sorely tempted to ban all April Fools' pranks, but the students enjoyed them so much. At least Ethan wouldn't be there the following year, she reminded herself.

"Ethan, can you perform a dissolution spell?" Professor Powell asked.

"Sometimes?"

Kathleen rolled her eyes. "I can do them. Will there be any credit in it?"

She held her hands up when she saw the dark looks on the professors' faces.

"Joking."

Kathleen called her magic and formed the dissolution spell. The web shredded from the center outward and fluttered away on an invisible breeze.

"Come on, Ethan, time to learn." Professor Powell gestured down the hall. "You'll be an expert by the time you've finished."

Classes were an hour late, and the kitchen pixies refused to give Ethan anything but dry toast as punishment for ruining their carefully prepared breakfast. No one spoke to him. Some of the freshmen did, however, cast a spell on him. Glittery goo coated his hair and dripped down his pajama bottoms. A sophomore turned his hair neon-pink with small baby blue bows that he couldn't remove no matter how hard he tried.

Despite it all, Ethan felt a great swell of pride as he tried to scrub his hair clean. The doorway prank had been the best yet.

CHAPTER FOURTEEN

" Can you believe what a foul mood Cooper was in this morning?" Peter took his usual seat. "He practically took Tia's head off."

Emma nudged her bag beneath her seat. "Everyone seems to be on edge this week. Did you hear that the dead animals are back?"

Alison frowned. It had been a while since they'd heard anything about that. People had shrugged it off as a weird disease or a particularly harsh winter. For a while, everything had almost felt normal.

"Are they small animals like before?" Aya took a bite from her sandwich. "Or?"

"I think it started this morning. Someone said a bunch of frogs were found near the barn." Emma picked at her salad. "That's a long way from the stream."

Kathleen ignored the conversation in favor of watching Professor Heineken enter the room. She wasn't the only one. He had quite a fan club, Alison noted. He seemed to be talking to himself, and his hands moved in small, precise gestures. A deep frown formed on his face and created wrinkles around his eyes.

"I bet he's trying to figure out something really complicated." Kathleen nibbled at her sandwich. "I'm sure it'll transform the world of magic and mechanics."

Tanner wanted to say something biting but held his tongue. His morning hadn't been great and setting Kathleen off wouldn't help any.

Alison watched as Professor Heineken went to sit with the other professors but changed his mind at the last second. He stood and left the room. Tanner put his hand on her thigh and looked pointedly at her sandwich made of bread not long out the oven. The pixies would be upset if she left that.

"You can't start skipping meals to chase down possible mysteries. He's probably running through a test he plans on giving later." He smiled gently.

Jason hadn't given up on his quest to find out what was going on at the school but he hadn't succeeded in entering Professor Heineken's cottage. The one time he had gone there had taken him two hours of carefully planned movements and stealth spells. When he finally reached it, he found the dwelling was locked down tighter than a gnome's bank vault.

He noticed the professor acting weird and wolfed down the last of his beef sandwich before stalking him through the hallways until he stopped beneath the wide staircase.

Jason pressed himself against the wall and cast a small look-away spell to hide himself.

———

Ira swallowed hard. His latest experiment had gone awry. He had transferred the power from the kemana crystal into himself, but at great cost. The magic in his system had fizzled and burned out within twelve hours. Worse, he knew that he had drawn the attention of something dark and malicious. That wasn't the only downside. The remnants of the new magic had altered his. Now, it escaped his grasp and wandered free as wild shards, totally uncontrolled.

He whispered a spell and tried to weave his power to contain the remnants of the wild force freed by his experiment. The sharp slivers of pure magic that would quickly draw attention.

Closing his eyes, he focused on the tiny scraps of his magic buried within that wildness. He chanted and tugged it back to where it belonged. This was the third time this month he'd had to retrieve it, and it was getting worse. He needed more magic from the kemana crystal. That was the only way to stitch himself back together. Ira knew he was close now. He could feel it.

Once his magic returned, Ira opened his eyes and tensed. The darkness was watching him. A sharp prickle traced down his back as his instincts told him to run.

Professor Hudson came around the corner and smiled gently at him. "Is everything okay, Ira?"

"I think something dark is following me."

She paused mid-step, saw the shadows under his eyes, and noticed that he'd lost some weight. He was always working on one thing or another.

"Perhaps you should visit the infirmary. You do look exhausted."

Ira nodded and smiled. "I haven't been sleeping well. Maybe they can make me a draught."

Peter dragged his fingers through his hair. "I really hope this is an easy class. I'm too tired to focus. The project for Entrepreneurs Club has been difficult."

"I'm sorry to disappoint you, but you will not, in fact, nap through this class." Professor Regency glared at Peter. "I will, however, make sure to call you first when I need volunteers."

Peter had the good sense not to say anything and slid into his seat next to Ethan.

Professor Regency held his glass of whiskey in his hand and ignored the desire to partake. It had already been a long week.

He looked around the room. "Today, the subject is weapons. You will channel the appropriate elemental magics and form them into solid, usable weapons."

Alison was over the moon to hear this. She'd read that Drow magic was particularly good for that. There would be times as a bounty hunter when she wouldn't have a weapon on her, so the ability to form one from scratch would be incredibly useful.

Whispers broke out slowly around the room, and Professor Regency took a small sip of his whiskey.

"We'll begin with Peter, who so kindly volunteered a minute ago. Come up to the front of the class and show us how it's done."

Peter dragged his feet a little. This hadn't been his specialty for all four years. He ran the forms of magic through his mind, trying to think which would work to create a small dagger. The visualization was solid in his mind when he turned to face the class. Channeling wasn't his strongest suit, but he wouldn't be humiliated.

He reached into his deepest essence and held the image and feel of the small dagger in focus. Slowly, the magic crept through his fingertips. His wand remained on his desk. The point was to be able to call enchantment through other means than the usual, after all.

Carefully, he compressed his power and tried to hone it into a sharp point. Adding a touch of earth magic from somewhere beneath his feet, he encouraged it to give his dagger solidity. He opened his eyes to find a small knife in the palm of his hand. It was more like a rough shiv than a neat dagger, but it was enough to satisfy Professor Regency.

Alison was eager and took her turn next. Her magic rushed forward, almost overwhelming her. She took a deep breath and pulled it under control. Once the power was more malleable beneath her fingertips, she wasted no time creating a pitch-black dagger with a long, slender blade and a deep-blue hilt. Her Drow abilities had been developing nicely.

A few mutters about showing off rippled through the

room, but mostly, people were impressed, including Professor Regency.

Then, it was Emma's turn. She walked to the front of the room and reminded herself that she'd practiced her channeling. It was only one small knife. No big deal. She pulled her magic, but something much darker and dangerous invaded her mind and slid around inside her. She gasped as the sharp edge of something bit into the palm of her hand.

Try as she might, Emma couldn't regain control. Everything turned pitch-black, her throat constricted, and her heart hammered in her chest. The class watched in horror as pitch-black points formed from Emma's hand and continuously multiplied and morphed into wicked-edged knives.

Professor Regency placed his whiskey down and identified where she was channeling from. He reached out with his magic and closed a small rift that she had somehow managed to open to the darkness of the World in Between. He frowned as he realized that there was no trace of her magic on the rift. It had opened of its own accord.

Emma fell to her knees and tried desperately to calm herself before she became more of a talking point around the school. There was no explanation for the situation. She had channeled magic hundreds of times before, and nothing like that had ever happened.

Professor Regency helped her to her feet, but she refused to go to the infirmary. Kathleen and Aya fussed over her when she sat down but all she wanted to do was vanish and pretend none of it was real.

The professor decided to focus the class on channeling

fire and light magic alternately so they could feel the difference and not set themselves ablaze when they tried to form a light. Emma remained quiet and withdrawn, reluctant to call on her magic again in case the darkness returned. It had gone, but she didn't feel safe.

CHAPTER FIFTEEN

Professor Grant held her hand up before the students could get too comfortable.

"We're taking a field trip to the kemana today."

"Fantastic—shopping."

"We can practice our fireballs."

"We're going to study the large crystal at the center. We will discuss it and then take the train to the Pleasantville kemana." Professor Grant fixed the group with a firm look. "You can go shopping on your own time."

She hoped that she wouldn't regret this field trip. The students were usually well-behaved, but the kemana offered a bigger distraction than most places. She ushered them out of the school and headed for the stairway.

Annabelle hadn't visited there in a few months. She'd been busy completing a journal article on the crystal in Pleasantville. She knew something was wrong the moment she stepped onto the stairs. The lights that usually surrounded them were dull, and once they'd reached the bottom, the residents seemed less. The entire place had a distinctly subdued feel to it. Professor Grant pursed her lips and tried to see if there was a clear source of the problems.

A pair of students attempted to slip away down one of the side streets, no doubt for a quick shopping trip. Professor Grant called them back and herded the group directly to the crystal. Perhaps she'd be able to find the source of the problems there.

Alison felt something watching her. She looked around and didn't see anyone besides her usual friends and classmates. The shop owners were all hidden within the confines of their stores, and the usual bustle of business was absent. When she pulled her glasses off to study the magic, she noted that it lacked a lot of the vibrancy she'd seen in the past. The usual vivid technicolor display of power was faded and almost broken in some places.

She examined the ground, trying to pinpoint exactly where the problems stemmed from, when she saw a little ball of bright orange magic. Alison put her glasses back on and saw the little salamander she'd seen at the Ifrit store following her. The small crystal lizard ducked into the shadows of a shop, but it was too late. She had spotted it.

The creature continued its pursuit past bookstores and food stalls. It remained ten feet from her no matter what her pace or which side of the street she walked on. Alison's curiosity had been piqued. She paused and grabbed the salamander. Its bright orange magic flared to an almost blinding white before it subsided and became a dead crystal ornament entirely devoid of magic.

"So, whoever enchanted it included a trigger to remove its magic when it was caught," Alison mused.

"Did you say something?" Aya looked from her to the salamander.

"Where did that come from?"

"It was following me."

Professor Grant raised an eyebrow and took the artifact from Alison. She pursed her lips and sighed. "You upset an Ifrit at some point. This was intended to stalk you so the Ifrit could take what it felt was its due. They're a common issue. I recommend you don't go near the Ifrit again."

Kathleen looked at the salamander. "It'd make a pretty paperweight."

Professor Grant dropped it in the closest trash can.

"It'll disintegrate into a pile of dust within the hour."

They reached the large crystal at the heart of the kemana and found it, too, lacked much of its usual glow.

Professor Grant frowned and reached out to feel the magic that always lapped against her palm. It wasn't present. Someone or something had drained the crystal. She made a mental note to do some research into how that was possible and who might have a possible motive.

Alison saw the expression on the woman's face and knew that she had a mystery to solve. Something had harmed the crystal, which meant that the school was now vulnerable. Did that have something to do with the dead animals?

"As you can see, this crystal is the heart of the kemana. It also fuels the defenses within our school and grounds. These crystals can be found at the heart of every kemana around the world. They're an integral part of our society."

Professor Grant was unnerved and didn't have the heart to continue her talk. She sent the students back to the school so they could board Mrs. Beasley's jitney. She slid one final glance to the crystal and frowned. Something was incredibly wrong.

The students hadn't paid much attention. They were far more interested in seeing the Pleasantville kemana.

"It's beneath New York."

"Think of the fashion potential." Kathleen leaned between the seats so she could talk to Alison and Tanner. "I can't believe she won't let us do a little shopping at least. That's cruel. Who cares about the stupid crystal anyway?"

Alison looked out the window. "It is very important to the safety of the school and the inhabitants of the kemana and something we should know."

They bustled through the Starbucks to the train station. The commuters didn't look very pleased to have the car full of loud students.

"I've never been to New York. We should do a trip there sometime." Emma looked at her friends. "All of us. When we're in college, we can meet up and do a weekend in New York."

Aya beamed. "That sounds like a great idea. It's perfect for adventures."

"We'll see how busy I am." Kathleen looked at herself in a small mirror. "If I have enough time in my schedule then I'd love to."

Luke tried to keep his tone even. "You'll be in New York anyway, so it's not as if it'll be a struggle for you."

Kathleen ignored him. Her dislike had only become

clearer over the months that had passed. Luke huffed and folded his arms.

Professor Grant did her best to keep the students together, but there was always one straggler somewhere. Her mind was on the Ruby Falls' crystal, and she almost missed the turn down to the Pleasantville one.

To her relief, that kemana was as full of life and as busy as she remembered. The students made their way through the crowds of shoppers and between the brightly colored shops and stalls selling everything one could possibly imagine.

Alison wanted to stop and look at a stall that sold every shape and form of keys. She saw the magic wrapped around them but didn't know their purpose.

"Come on, Miss Brownstone. We are on a schedule," Professor Grant called.

Tanner squeezed her hand, and they walked with Luke who looked forlorn again. Aya and Kathleen whispered and looked back at him. The shifter tried to ignore it and thought about Louper and his grades instead, but having his friends turn against him hurt. He hadn't done anything wrong. Apparently, even having the potential to was good enough for them.

Alison joined the rest of the students as they crowded around the brilliant white crystal at the heart of the kemana. Professor Grant began her lecture on the crystal's magic and its importance. Alison only half listened as she tried to decide how best to approach the problem of the Ruby Falls' crystal that had clearly been depleted. It could be the beginning of another attack on the school, and she couldn't allow that to happen.

Alison and her friends returned to the local kemana that evening. They had planned on playing around with their magic, but Alison noticed that Professor Heineken was down there, looking very shady. She let her friends go on without her as she called her magic and shrouded herself in shadow. It felt strange against her skin, comforting and yet oddly physical like cool silk. She used the darkness at the edges of the street to follow the professor, curious to see what he was doing.

Ira needed to speak to his contact again. Something was very wrong with his experiments. He had succeeded in tapping into the crystal and had drained some of the magic, but it didn't flow as it should. It kept disintegrating and unraveling around him. His own magic grew increasingly erratic, and the nightmares—he couldn't bear to think about those.

Something was following him. Ira paused and glanced back, trying to pinpoint the source of the prickling feeling. It was nearly always present now, just out of sight, but he could feel it. He drew himself a little taller and ducked into the small space between the shops where Melchior insisted on meeting.

A pair of vertebrae had joined the other bone shards around the edge of the area, reminders of what happened to people who got on Melchior's bad side. The grizzled man stepped in when Ira was beginning to think that he wasn't coming. His usual pair of shifters closed off the escape route. He'd been there enough times to know how this worked.

"And what can I do for you today?" Melchior licked his lips. "You have the appropriate payment, I assume."

Ira bit back a sigh of frustration and held out three vials of dragon's blood. He'd had to use a heavy sleeping spell on the dragon to draw those. Their blood was incredibly potent and rare, and he didn't want to know what someone like Melchior would do with it.

"It isn't working. The crystal is supposed to work with my magic to make me more powerful. Instead, mine is becoming volatile, and I can't contain the crystal magic. I need to get to the heart of it."

Melchior slowly raised an eyebrow.

"Do you take me for a complete fool? This is my home."

"I'm close. I know I'm close," Ira pleaded.

"You're an addict," Melchior snarled.

Ira took a step back in horror at that idea. He wasn't an addict.

"Leave here. You will not go any deeper into the crystal."

"But—"

Melchior held up his hand, and his shifters moved closer.

Ira nodded and left without another word. No good came from arguing with someone like him. He needed a stronger ally who could give him what he needed. If he could reach the heart of the crystal, he could resolve all his problems. He knew it. With one more vial of the kemana magic—the true heart magic— everything would fall into place. He was on the precipice of greatness.

Alison had heard everything. She trailed Professor Heineken back to the stairs and saw something odd that wasn't there with her glasses. When she crept closer, she saw it was Jason Parker, wrapped in a stealth spell and a complicated one at that. He followed the professor up the stairs. Alison wasn't sure what he was up to, but she had no doubt it involved dark magic.

She jogged down the familiar streets and found Tanner and Luke standing outside an expensive boutique which must have been Kathleen's choice.

"Is everything okay?" Tanner took her hand. "You're out of breath."

She smiled before she shook her head.

"I saw Professor Heineken acting strange, so I followed him." She slowed her breathing. "He's in some really deep trouble. He talked to a dangerous-looking man about taking the magic from the crystal."

Peter emerged from the shop. "Who took the magic from the crystal? You're sure?"

"Yes. Professor Heineken has been draining it to make himself more powerful. He acted like an addict. You should have seen him. He couldn't stand still and was really agitated when the criminal wouldn't let him take more." Alison wished she'd been able to record it to show her friends. "I don't think he'll stop."

"You can't screw with the kemana crystals. If you poke

too hard, they go kaboom. And it won't take out only the kemana or the school. It could destroy the entire state." Peter swallowed hard.

"What could destroy the entire state?" Emma looked at the gathered friends as the others exited the store behind her. "Are you playing with insane inventions again, Peter?"

"Professor Heineken has been draining the crystal. He's putting everyone at risk." Alison tried to keep her tone even, but she grew tired of repeating herself. "He won't stop."

Ethan shrugged. "Then we stop him. Isn't that what we do?"

Alison smiled, feeling better now that her friends were on board.

"What about the professors? Shouldn't we tell them? I mean, he is one of them." Aya frowned.

"We have no proof." Kathleen pursed her lips. "They'd never believe us. They'll close ranks around their colleague."

Alison wouldn't have put it quite like that, but she believed that would be the case. She had no proof. It was her word against a professor's.

"I'm not sure. You could have misunderstood," Aya said softly.

Alison folded her arms. "He took three vials of Dorvu's blood to pay the man. An innocent man wouldn't steal his blood. And I saw Jason Parker following him."

Aya's eyes went wide. "Dragon's blood is dangerous. And we all know Jason Parker only deals in dark magic."

Tanner looked at his friends. "So, we're doing this? We're taking down this professor and saving the day?"

Luke put his hand into the middle of the group. "We need some sort of cool slogan."

Tanner, Alison, and Peter all bumped fists with Luke. The others rolled their eyes or pretended it wasn't happening. Alison had to admit it was dorky, but something about it felt good.

CHAPTER SIXTEEN

Peter and Ella pushed the music magic slowly into the delicate butterflies. They had started with a small handful—only ten brightly colored butterflies—but they were confident this would work beautifully and they could begin selling them by the end of the week.

"We'll rock this final project." Adam jotted down potential pitches to use on the clubs. "We'll go down in the books."

Ella frowned and ignored him as she placed the final note of the techno music into the bright red wing of the butterfly.

"Where shall we try them out? In here?" Peter asked, looking at the group.

Adam shrugged, and Ella picked up a couple of the butterflies. They had been painstakingly made by hand. Each tiny twist of copper wire and brightly colored silk had taken them hours. They were a true work of art, though. Each was unique in appearance, and with music, it was a great selling point. They hoped that they would become collectors' items once the music ran out, making them worth even more.

The butterflies fluttered their wings, and soft sounds of techno and electronic music could be heard if Peter strained to listen. The music was in there, which was a great start. The original butterfly project had worked beautifully and entertained the students for hours. Now, it was time to try the final product.

"If we release one in each corner, we can see how they sync up." Ella pointed to the corners. "They should provide different moods which will appeal to the larger clubs. We need to make sure the music doesn't overlap and clash with the other areas, though."

They each took a single butterfly and moved to a different corner. Peter stood with his back against the wall and a large window looking over the rolling green lawns out the front of the school.

"On three." Ella lifted hers. "One. Two. Three."

They threw their butterflies gently into the air which had been programmed to act as the trigger. Adam was satisfied that it was clear enough, but they would work on that once they'd made sure the music synced together.

Peter's butterfly, a sea-blue and emerald-green speckled design with delicate, almost translucent segmented wings, flew directly up to the ceiling. Its wings fluttered as it hovered in the one spot. He frowned. Where was the music?

Suddenly, music filled the room. It deafened the students, and the furniture around them rattled and shook. The walls trembled, and the music only increased in volume.

It was a cacophony that made Peter curl in on himself as he tried to protect his head. The damp, sticky feeling of blood surrounded his ears and nose, and the sound grew louder.

The desks and chairs splintered and broke. A large crack formed in one wall and the floor tiles began to rise. Then, suddenly, it was over. Agonizing silence descended, and Peter felt as though someone had stolen the air from his lungs.

When he could breathe again, he raised his head and saw a furious headmistress and Professor Grant looking at them.

"What on Earth did you think you were playing at? You are supposed to be entrepreneurs not..." she searched for a good word, "destructive magicians."

Peter looked around at the thin layer of plaster dust that covered the broken remains of the furniture and the warped tiles around him. Ella raised her eyes and released a pitiful cough.

"We're working on our final project." Peter uncurled himself. "We put electronic music into magical butterflies. We planned to sell them to the dance clubs."

The headmistress narrowed her eyes.

"Do you have any idea how much damage you have done? Or how many people you could have hurt?"

"No—"

"Go to the infirmary. That is a nasty nosebleed." She pointed out the door "We will discuss the possibility of you continuing this project tomorrow."

Peter's heart dropped into his shoes. He had spent months perfecting those butterflies and the music. He'd planned to use the money to help pay his college fees, and it was all slipping between his fingers.

Things only got worse when word spread through school about what had happened. Peter walked into the dining hall only to have all eyes turn to him and all conversations stop dead. The expressions on the students' faces were dark at best and livid at worse. He'd seen some of them in the infirmary after furniture had broken or small pieces of architecture had fallen on them.

A red-headed elf stood up. "Technology has no place with magic. Every time it's been tried, bad things happened. You should stop screwing around with things that should not exist."

"It was a ridiculous idea." A wizard walked toward Peter. "No true wizard would be seen dead trying to mix the two."

"Plenty of wizards and witches have mixed the two. Elves have done it too," said Peter, lifting his chin.

"Look where it got us. The humans hated us more than ever. We should have stuck to what is ours and is special. You shouldn't be here if you want to play with human toys," A Light Elf scolded, pointing at him.

Peter tried to ignore it, but they only got louder. More people began telling him that magic and technology had no place together and that he was an idiot for even considering it. Some of them told him he was a traitor to the magical community. When he sat down, some students finally stood and began arguing that they were in the modern world and the potential was too great to ignore.

"You cannot hide in the past and cling onto segregation of magic and technology because of a few bad acts."

"We need to rely on what's always worked. The old ways. And that's magic in its pure form."

"There is too much potential to ignore the great things that could be brought into the world by combining magic and technology. Not everything that's happened has been negative."

"Too bad that the negative turned out to sometimes be deadly. How much do you sacrifice before you finally learn."

Peter's friends didn't say a word. Luke patted him on the back and gave him a gentle smile while the rest of the school shouted around them.

Finally, the pixies and professors reached their limit. One of the pixies used an amplification spell. "If you do not stop shouting right this second, I will take your dinner away and you will have dry toast for breakfast tomorrow."

Everyone sat down and fell silent.

Mara Berens stepped forward and drew in a deep breath, gathering her thoughts. "Clearly, we have all gotten distracted in the past and forgotten some of the mission of this particular school. The entire purpose of the School of Necessary Magic is to get ready to integrate the magical and the mundane. I don't condone the irresponsible mixing of magic and tech, but it is inevitable and ultimately necessary. As a small, furry friend of mine would say, minus the swearing, get over yourselves and get on with things."

***

Tanner borrowed the Chevette and surprised Alison with a

date night in Charlottesville. It had been a while since they'd had an evening to themselves, and with the future looming, the time felt right. Alison looked around at the brightly colored town with the fresh bursts of flowers and green growth on the trees and smiled. Summer was right around the corner, and spring was at its peak.

Tanner slipped his arm around her waist, and they walked down the sidewalk in a comfortable silence. The warm air was the perfect temperature, and the birds sang as they settled for the evening. He had chosen a pleasant restaurant for them to enjoy a quiet meal. It wasn't anything too fancy, though. He was still a student after all.

They sat at a small, dark, wooden table in the corner. The trio of tealights in the center added a little romance to the scene. Soft string music played over hidden speakers as they studied their menus.

"We don't have long left at school." Tanner closed his menu. "College seems really close now."

"It's not long until finals. How do you feel about your chances of getting into the medical course at Georgetown?"

The waitress arrived to take their orders. They each opted for a chicken dish and soda.

He entwined his fingers with Alison's. "I feel pretty good. My grades are high. I'm in the top ten percent of all my classes, and I want to make a difference, you know? I want to make the world a little brighter."

Alison saw the warm glow of affection in Tanner's soul and smiled. He had a good heart and such strength. That was what had drawn her to him in the first place.

"I'm sure you'll be amazing. Any idea what your focus will be?"

"Pediatrics appeals right now. It's rough having a childhood illness. If I can help those kids, I think it'd be amazing. I'm considering neurology, too. It's an absolutely fascinating subject, and it can intersect with magic."

Alison subtly cast a small spell to stop eavesdroppers before they continued the discussion.

"I've heard they're making inroads with magic and medicine. Maybe you can be on the front line for that."

Tanner grinned. "Think of the progress we could make if we could pull that off. And the suffering that could be prevented. I'd like to study non-human medicine, too. I think that's something that's overlooked. It leans so heavily on magic right now, but the advances we could make are incredible."

Tanner's enthusiasm and passion were contagious. Alison smiled and reveled in it. He rubbed his thumb along the edge of her hand.

"We could make it work, you know, if you wanted to. It wouldn't be easy, but once I'm trained, I might be able to work as a mobile medic."

Alison squeezed his hand. "What about your dreams to be a pediatrician? Or a neurologist? You need to be based in a hospital for those."

"I could focus more on research. If I wandered the country with you, I could speak with the non-human communities and bring together the knowledge from those."

"Don't give up your dreams for me." Alison tried to be gentle. "You need to live for yourself."

Tanner smiled, and to Alison's relief, there were no signs of offense or distress in his soul.

"We have college still, so who knows what will change? I just...I'd like us to have a chance."

Alison took a sip of her drink. "There are many years ahead of us. We'll do what we can to make each other happy. The future is bright."

They ate their meal in relative quiet, and the conversation turned to more comfortable topics.

"Have you prepped for the potions final? I think she'll slip in something obscure to make us really work. Maybe a luck potion." Tanner finished his last bite.

"We should arrange a library study session this week. We'll dig out the unusual potions and make sure we're familiar with them."

He grinned. "Any excuse to read. I'm sure you already know all the potions anyway. It's history I'm worried about. I can't make all those dates stick in my head."

Alison wrinkled her nose. "You know there will be so many dates on that exam."

"There's more to history than dates. I mean, as long as we get the facts straight, is it the end of the world if we're a year or two off?"

Alison laughed. "I suppose we'll find out."

As they walked back to the car, they heard the wolves howling in the distance. She thought of Izzie and hoped that she was happy wherever she was. Luke clearly missed her dearly.

CHAPTER SEVENTEEN

L uke looked around his team and felt confident. They were up against the Atlantic City Seagulls, and he knew they could beat them. They had trained hard as a team, their stamina was much better, and they had some fresh spells under their belt. Etienne had perfected a few tracking spells to avoid wasting time going in the wrong direction. Cody and Daniel had focused their efforts on defense spells, including shields. Matt and Luke had trained physically as much as they could. Together, they were unstoppable. Luke was sure of it.

The crowd stood and greeted them with a roar of applause when they walked out onto the field. Cody and Daniel made big bows and grinned, loving the attention. Coach Regency lifted his glass of whiskey to them, a small show of confidence.

"Remember, we're unstoppable," Luke told his teammates.

He rolled his shoulders and prepared mentally. The

Seagulls were a strong team. They had a fast captain, but he and Matt were better.

The scene descended, and the team found themselves inside a large, high-ceilinged building. The pale, cream floors shone under bright artificial lights. More marble covered the walls and formed large pillars and a wide, sweeping staircase. Etienne whispered and formed the simple tracking spell. A bright purple arrow appeared ahead and vibrated, urging them to move.

They jogged across the marble floor and turned the corner into a new room. Paintings of people dressed in weird, old-fashioned clothes were evenly spaced along the high walls. Luke still had no idea where they were.

The arrow moved into the room on the right. They skidded on the slippery surface and almost crashed into a large stuffed Kodiak bear.

"We're in a natural history museum!" Matt exclaimed, looking warily at the bear. "I think it's really creepy the way they stuff animals."

A low growl came from their left. The pride of lions that had been motionless in front of a pretty savannah scene a moment ago stared at them with glass eyes.

Cody looked at Luke. "What do we do? Run or immobilize?"

"Freeze them so we can get moving." Luke looked at the arrow which twitched violently. "Like we practiced."

Cody and Daniel drew their wands. They worked as a pair, a well-oiled machine. The lions stepped from their display with murderous intent but immediately froze. The wizards high-fived each other before everyone raced after the arrow once again.

They ran through rooms with stuffed animals from every biome. Tigers watched them from behind thick glass, and crocodiles snapped at their ankles as they rushed by. Cody watched in alarm as one reptile pushed onto its feet and gave chase. He had thought they were slow-moving water predators, but the mass of teeth and armor gained on them. They turned the corner, and the click of its sharp claws became a high-pitched squeal when it lost its footing and skidded across the marble into a honey badger's display case.

The pair of badgers made the most of the display's new hole and bolted toward the team. The crowd gasped as the small, dark murder machines gained on them with every step.

"Honey badgers are one of the most vicious animals," Emma whispered, unable to look away. "Although I'd still choose one over an angry kitchen pixie."

Etienne slowed his steps and spun with a feral grin on his face. He lowered into a fighting stance and held his hands palm out toward the attackers. Their low-slung bodies made it difficult to target their throat or stomach, but the elf had a different plan. He pushed a great wave of air toward them and they blasted back with furious hisses and growls.

The arrow guided the group up broad stairs that wound around the back wall of the building. Large windows looked out over an old city and heavy rain cascaded down the glass. Luke frowned when he caught an odd scent. It smelled dark and slightly damp. Matt caught it, too.

They were led into a dimly lit room where hiero-glyphics adorned the walls and canopic jars stood on display in the center of the room. Thick, heavy music pulsed through the space, sending shivers down their spines. It spoke of death and priests who weren't necessarily on your side.

Right on cue, a trio of men with tight, dark skin, sunken cheeks, and long, bony fingers stepped out of the darkness. They bore the costumes and markings of old Egyptian priests. Vicious tools appeared in their hands—sharp tools traditionally used to remove the internal organs before embalming.

"I don't know about you, guys, but I prefer my organs to remain inside." Matt eyed the approaching priests. "Plan of attack?"

"We tackle them and keep going." Luke could hear the footsteps of the rival team. "Now."

Luke and Matt charged the priests with their bodies low. The men looked bemused right before the shifters tackled them around the waist and drove them to the ground. The third went to plunge a sharp hook into Luke's back, but Etienne had summoned his sword and decapitated him. Matt jumped back from the leathery skull as it rolled and almost touched him.

Luke got back to his feet. "The Seagulls are nearby. We need to get going. Where's the arrow?"

They caught sight of the purple glow disappearing into the gloom of the next room. The scent of darkness and ill intent filled the entire space. There were no lights, and the music had stopped. The team slowed to a cautious walk as they explored the area, waiting for the next trap. The arrow hovered at the far side.

Movement caught Luke's attention. Someone or something crept around them. His night vision wasn't good enough to identify more than a broad-shouldered silhouette. It was truly pitch-black in there.

The three magical members tried to cast light spells, but none worked. They spluttered and died rather than forming even a simple flame. The sense of something very wrong filled Luke's gut, and he prepared to fight—to really fight.

His wolf side surged forward, and the silhouette was on him. Heavy fists punched his ribs and swept his legs out from under him. He should have been out of the game, but still, he remained in the darkness.

"Something's wrong." Alison watched in horror. "Why hasn't he been dropped?"

A concerned whisper spread through the crowd as they watched the team try to tear the silhouette off Luke. None of them could get a grip on it as the shifter fought with everything he had. He shrieked in agony, and finally, he dropped free.

In the field, he lay on his side, holding his right arm to his chest. His breathing came in ragged bursts as he tried to focus past the pain. He could feel that his wrist was shattered.

The medics ran forward. Alison and her friends tried to push through the crowd to reach him. That shouldn't have happened.

"What went wrong?" Alison glared at Coach Regency. "How did that happen?"

The gnome knocked his whiskey back. Usually, he never drank more than a small sip, but after seeing what happened to that poor shifter, he needed the warm burn.

He had no idea what had gone wrong, but someone had targeted Luke.

The medics lifted him gently to his feet and tried to look at his wrist. He held it close and growled at them. The pain was unlike anything he'd felt before. Finally, Alison and Tanner made it to his side. Tanner put his hand on Luke's shoulder, and Alison stood tall and strong with a stern glare on her face. She made it very clear that if anyone so much as looked at Luke funny, she'd make them suffer for it.

They examined his wrist and confirmed his fears. It was shattered and would take months to heal.

Tanner clenched his fist. "We can try a healing spell, fix you up in no time."

One of the medics shook his head. "Doesn't work on shifters. Something about the mix of human DNA and shifter."

"I can't run with my pack," he whispered, holding back the tears.

For the first time in a long time, he felt truly lost.

CHAPTER EIGHTEEN

I ra hid in his office. Everyone had been summoned to the auditorium, but he needed to breathe. He'd found someone else to work with in his quest and Melchior had been found dead the day before. Sara was far more dangerous than he had dreamed when he'd first cut a deal with her.

He paced in front of his desk with the last vial of the kemana crystal's magic in his hand. He needed a little taste to get him through the day. It wasn't such a big deal and he was so close to success. His magic had almost fled him entirely, but he could feel the crystal's magic in his veins. It had been difficult at first and it had left its mark on him, but he was stronger for it. He swallowed hard.

"Just a little taste."

That was his last vial. The next experiment had to be the final one. There was no more after that, or so Sara had told him. He was working on a way to convince her, though. He was too close to stop now. The brotherhood would be proud of him and he would be raised up as a savior.

He pulled the stopper from the vial and ran his tongue over the edge. The sweet bliss of the magic filled his system, and he felt alive again. The darkness hovered and he could feel its eyes on him. Each sweet sip of magic brought it a step closer until it was almost within arm's reach. It invaded his dreams, turning them into chaotic nightmares of death and destruction.

Ira smoothed a hand down his clothes, then hid the vial in his desk. Everything was fine. He simply needed to smile politely and get through the talk in the auditorium.

When he stepped out of his office, he saw Jason Parker at the end of the hallway, leaning casually against the wall and smiling at him. The student was becoming a problem in Ira's life. Everywhere he turned, Jason was there, watching him. The professor was sure the boy had tried to break into his cottage twice. Thankfully, he hadn't succeeded, but Jason must be after the magic. His family would be overjoyed to have such power under their control. Ira would have to remove him from the equation soon. First, though, he had to get through this talk.

Alison and Tanner filed into the auditorium behind Kathleen and the others. The headmistress had canceled the class before lunch and summoned the entire school. They settled and waited as Headmistress Berens stepped to the front.

"I have called you all here today because a chasm has

formed within the school body." She looked around. "There have been fights, bullying, and more, and all over the role of magic and technology. Today, we will resolve this issue and move forward in a positive fashion."

A freshman Light Elf stood up. The headmistress nodded and weaved a spell to make sure everyone heard what the student said.

"Magic and technology do not and cannot mix. Magicals are separate and distinct from humans. It is to our benefit that we remain that way."

She sat down having said all she had to say on the matter.

A half-blooded witch stood. "The world and society cannot progress if we don't allow for evolution."

The students muttered amongst themselves. A feeling of explosive conflict swelled and filled the air with unseen electricity. Peter kept his head down. He and his Entrepreneur's Club had started this. They'd had verbal abuse thrown at them in the corridors and had been pushed out of other social circles, and all because of one small accident.

Alison stood and walked slowly to the front. A hush settled as those gathered waited to see what the Drow would do. Everyone knew what she was even if they didn't know details. There were rumors about her involvement in the dead animals and the big fight against the dark magic users.

She stood near Ms. Berens and waited for quiet while she arranged her thoughts in her mind.

"We are in an important era within our society, and all important times bring discomfort and conflict. We have traditionally been hidden from the humans for fear of what would happen to both them and us. This has led to a separation of magic and human technology. As technology has grown and progressed, it has shown great potential for the evolution and advancement of society as a whole.

"This could benefit everyone. It is time we stopped viewing this situation as us versus them. Humans are people, the same as we are. We can wield magic and they can't, but that doesn't make them some foreign creature too alien for us to interact with. They are scared of us because of what we can do. And here we are, too scared of the potential they hold to step up and offer them the opportunity to unite and progress with us."

She glanced around at the students and professors.

"It is down to us, to our generation, to be the leaders our society needs. This is the time for us to go out into the world and show the humans that we are not something to be feared. We are here to help each other. Together, we can create something truly great. If we can combine technology and magic, we can reduce the suffering in the world, and who knows, maybe we can find new worlds to explore.

"Together, we are stronger."

The silence lasted for a couple of heartbeats. Alison wondered if she'd screwed this up. Ms. Berens started clapping, and soon, everyone joined her. Alison smiled with relief.

"Well said, Miss Brownstone."

Alison made her way back to her seat beside Tanner, who squeezed her hand and kissed her cheek.

"You're amazing, you know that?" he whispered.

"As Miss Brownstone said, it is time to put your concerns and differences aside. We need to come together to make this world a brighter place. There are far more dangerous foes out there."

"Like dark magic?"

"Yes. Like dark magic."

Xander caught his name among the whispers and fought to maintain the polite smile. That was a stain that would forever remain on his name but he didn't regret it.

"The Entrepreneurs Club made a mistake. However, they were experimenting. They were working to form a new bridge between us and the human world around us. That is a goal we should all strive to achieve. From now on, there will be no more discussions on this subject. You will respect each other."

A murmur of agreement passed through the assembled students. Peter felt many eyes on him, but no one threw any magic or sharp objects at him, so he took it as a win. He would have preferred this be solved quietly rather than drawing more attention to him and his club, but if it meant he was free to wander the school again, he'd take it. And it felt good to be praised for building the bridge between magicals and humans.

CHAPTER NINETEEN

Alison paused to look out the window and admire the beautiful spring day. The green was particularly vibrant, and the flowerbeds burst with stunning flowers representing every color under the rainbow. She followed her friends to their usual table in the dining hall.

Luke had barely sat down when a muffin hit him on the back of the head. He looked around, trying to identify the culprit. His arm was still in a sling, and the fact he couldn't throw very well only reminded him that he was struggling in Louper training.

A warm, wet splat hit Christie in the middle of her forehead. Deep-red jam slid slowly down the bridge of her nose as she tried to clean it off. It became a free for all. Suddenly, food rocketed across the room. Eggs splattered against clothes. Sausages collided with backs and bounced across tables. Slices of toast became Frisbees as they spun through the air toward an unsuspecting target.

In an instant, it all vanished without a sound. Every scrap of food was gone. The students looked around in confusion. The pixies stood near the kitchen with thunderous expressions on their faces. As one, they flicked their wrists, and the food reappeared, all of it on a collision course with students. Alison ducked before a handful of warm oatmeal splatted on the floor behind her. Aya wasn't quite as quick and had milk and cornflakes dripping down her face and into the collar of her uniform. She coughed and spluttered.

The pixies all laughed before they returned to work.

"I don't think food fights are such a great idea." Luke picked scrambled eggs out of his hair. "How will we shower in time to get to class now?"

Everyone laughed as they looked at each other. They were all coated with some form of breakfast food or another. Kathleen had a glop of jam stuck to her cheek, and her hair was streaked with what looked like a cheesy omelet. Tanner picked pieces of bacon from his collar, and Aya tried to wipe the milk from her face.

As much as it was a complete mess, it had provided a tension breaker they desperately needed. They had final exams today, and none of them felt prepared.

Alison and Tanner had crammed for the Potions final all week. It had invaded her dreams, in which she ran from monstrous basil plants and found dusty handprints made from ground belladonna throughout her house. Plants didn't come naturally to her, but she'd given it her all.

Each student had been given their own small desk, and silence fell in the room. Professor Fowler was solemn as she placed the written portion of the test down on each desk. Once they had completed that section, they had thirty minutes to produce a scryer potion from the ingredients provided.

Emma squeezed her eyes closed. She knew she should have paid more attention to the obscure potions. Scrying potions were something a lot of people looked down on, and she had focused on the more useful potions like healing and obfuscation. She cursed under her breath and hoped it would come to her.

Alison looked at the written exam and tried to focus. She'd studied this time and again, and if she could remain calm, it would be a breeze. The first question completely threw her.

When dried forget-me-not is combined over flames with dried hyssop, what must you do first?

Alison's mind had gone completely blank. She knew that dried forget-me-not was often tied to memory spells, but hyssop focused more on cleansing. If they were combined over a flame, they needed igniting. She chewed her bottom lip and tried to puzzle it out. finally, she wrote that one must fan the flames to encourage the magic to rise. It felt right, but she had no idea if it was accurate.

Once she'd completed the written portion of the exam, Alison turned her full attention to the physical exam. The ingredients seemed vaguely familiar, and the mortar and pestle suggested that at least one of them needed grinding. She sat and looked at the magic within the herb for a few minutes before something clicked in her head and she knew exactly what she needed to do.

Professor Fowler tried to keep her expression blank as

she watched a few of the students mix the wrong ingredients. One of them, somehow, managed to set her dog rose leaves on fire. She had done her best to teach them, but some people didn't have the knack for plants and potions. She hoped they were more suited to other ventures.

The clock ticked, and she called time. A few of the students had barely begun their potion and had to be helped to stop it from boiling over and causing a disaster. Scrying wasn't easy to master, and it showed with some of the students' work. She had each student bottle up their potion, and she would grade them that afternoon.

Some of the bottles shined a bright leaf-green when it should have been a glittery purple-grey. Those were an immediate fail. Each student left the room with their head low and a look of defeat on their face. She had tried to make sure the exam was fair, but perhaps next year, she would go a little easier on the next class of students.

Still, these were the finals and each graduating class was supposed to be tested on everything they had learned at school.

Alison tried to clear her head before the transfiguration final with Professor Hodges.

"I'm sure he'll go easy on us." Kathleen smiled. "He likes us."

Peter skimmed his textbook while walking. "This is the final, so I'm sure he's not allowed to go easy on us. Do you think he'll go for biological or inanimate?"

"Inanimate. It has more use in the real world," Alison said.

Peter flipped through his textbook, trying to find the most difficult inanimate transfiguration workings. None of them were particularly easy. It was a tricky branch of magic that required the right mindset to pull it off. His head was still firmly on the final Entrepreneur Club project. They didn't have long to wrap it up, and he really wanted the money to go toward his college fund.

Professor Hodges ushered everyone into their seats. They were somehow late—every single one of them.

"As this is your final exam, you will do two workings. First, you will turn the pen and inkwell on your desks into a dagger and small shield."

He watched a look of abject horror cross some of the students' faces.

"Well, get started. You have a second working to do after this one."

As a shifter, Professor Hodges couldn't weave magic himself, but he knew transfiguration. He had been turning into a wolf his entire life after all.

Alison removed her glasses and focused on the simple, glossy black pen and small inkwell. No magic occurred naturally within them, which meant she was entirely on her own. That made it easier. If they contained magic, she would have to bend that to her will.

She began with the pen, since it was at least dagger-shaped. The image of a slender blade formed in her mind, and she reached out with her magic to feel the pen. Slowly, she molded her magic along its length and pushed it to extend and flatten. She tried to hold back the smile as it responded and the top became a small hilt. It was slow and tiring work, but she was close.

Ethan swallowed and ran his thumb over his focus bands, reminding himself that he could do this. He wrapped his hand around the inkwell and pictured it changing into a small, round shield. The words to aid his magic sprang to mind, and he whispered them in a slow, almost sultry chant. The object flattened in his hand and widened slowly. He kept his eyes closed and focused on the sensation of the shield forming and spreading across his palm. When he finally opened his eyes, a shield the size of a pancake sat where the inkwell had been. A grin filled his face.

Professor Hodges tried to remain neutral as he watched some of the less talented students warping their pens in weird and wonderful shapes. When the class was halfway over, he took the implements from everyone and jotted down the grades. Some of them would be very disappointed, but there was nothing he could do to change that.

"Now, you will transfigure this rose into a small songbird and back again."

Aya froze in her seat, panic overwhelming her. Kathleen reached across and squeezed her arm, easing the feeling of abject failure.

Professor Hodges placed a rose in front of each student and returned to his desk. He had stocked up on extra cleaning supplies for the test as there was a real risk of things getting very messy.

Alison saw the small threads of magic within the rose and tried to bend them to her will. They were stubborn and resisted her. She slowed her breathing and pushed aside the frustration, focusing instead on the sweet chirps of a small red songbird. The magic relented a little, and she managed to pull it outwards very slowly into something she could work with.

The red petals shriveled, and the stem shrank inwards. It became a twisted mess of color and textures as the feathers emerged, and finally, it turned into something bird-shaped. To Alison's disappointment, it had only one leg and its tail was crooked. Professor Hodges noted that down and watched as she returned the bird to a slightly crooked, misshapen rose. It wasn't perfect, but with her first transfiguration, she would still walk out with an A.

To the professor's surprise, Jason Parker performed both transfigurations with flying colors. The bright blue-and-yellow bird he formed was perfect and even chirped a few notes before he returned it to its original rose form. Jason hadn't shown any real desire to succeed in this class up until recently and the professor remained suspicious as to his intentions. He had heard that Jason had been seen around the staff offices a lot more than was usual.

Alison walked out of the transfiguration classroom feeling exhausted and ready to eat a gallon of ice-cream.

Kathleen looked at her. "How badly do you think you failed potions? I completely flunked. I don't care, though. You don't use potions in fashion."

"I feel pretty good about transfiguration." Alison frowned at the wood elf who pushed past her. "I'm not sure on potions. I think I got the actual potion's part okay, but the written part was a nightmare."

"I swear she didn't teach us half of that stuff. I certainly don't remember it," Peter complained, adjusting his bag.

"You have a head like a sieve. I'm not sure how you remember anything," Kathleen teased, grinning.

"Hey! I have a fantastic memory." Peter frowned. "Mostly."

Xander dragged his fingers through his hair. His past was coming back to haunt him. The problem was, he still wasn't entirely sure which part of his past it was. A shadowy figure had hung around the local area for a few weeks now. He knew he wasn't the only one to see it, but he hadn't been able to get a good look at or feel of them to know who it was. Unfortunately, his list of enemies was far longer than his arm, and that made life difficult.

There would be a time when he had no choice but to tell Mara. The figure had pushed onto school grounds, and it could have been him who broke Luke's arm. Xander couldn't be sure of any of it, though, and that pained him. He needed to act and soon, but first, he needed more information.

CHAPTER TWENTY

Peter looked at the trio of butterflies on the table in front of him. They needed to make them work. Otherwise, he'd fail, and he really couldn't afford to do that. The magic had been set in place, and they had discovered what caused the issue they had before. When they tried the four butterflies together, they'd missed the way the magic amplified each other's in an endless spiral. They hadn't noticed how the threads intersected. That had taken a month to fix, but they'd done it.

Now, they looked at the butterflies, wondering if they dared test them. Peter blew out a breath and picked up the emerald-green and snow-white butterfly.

"We have to do this. Then, we need to sell them." He looked at Ella. "Any news on the buyers?"

"Nothing until we prove they work."

"Do or die," Peter muttered.

They each took a butterfly and walked to the sides of the classroom. The cracks and damage had been repaired.

It had taken longer than anyone expected, but the room looked as good as new again.

Peter sent his butterfly up toward the ceiling. It fluttered its wings, and techno music played overhead. The other two butterflies were already in place, and nothing was shaking or exploding. Peter gave it five minutes before he walked toward Ella. He paused at a weird line where he could hear both songs playing at once. He took another step forward. The music from her butterfly had a much deeper bass with more synth.

They whooped and threw their hands up. They'd done it.

"Now we need to sell them." Adam reached for his butterfly. "We'll need to show the clubs that they work."

Ella looked at them. "Road trip? The professor has to say yes, right?"

"No. She doesn't." Professor Hudson looked at them with a stern expression. "You will conduct your business transactions from the school."

Adam gave her his most charming smile. "Don't you trust us?"

"No," Professor Hudson said flatly.

They began the tedious work of contacting the local clubs to tell them what they had. It was long and tiring, but they stuck with it. After the third hour, Peter felt his false smile would be stuck on his face permanently.

None of the club owners trusted someone who sounded so young or was from a strange school. They approached everyone they could reach within a fifty-mile radius and didn't get a single bite.

Alison and Tanner appeared in the doorway.

"How's it going?" She looked at their frazzled expressions. "That bad?"

Peter poked a butterfly. "We can't sell them, not a single one."

"Who's your target audience? Who have you contacted?" she asked, glancing at the butterflies.

"Clubs mostly, and a few bars." Adam rested his head on the table. "The usual dance places."

"What about college students?" Tanner looked at them. "I mean, they'll work for parties, right?"

Peter looked from Tanner to Alison, and a grin bloomed on his face.

He bounced up and hugged Tanner. "You're a freakin' genius. You should have joined us, dude."

Kathleen popped her head around the door.

"How's it going?"

"We have twenty-four hours to sell a minimum of twenty butterflies." Peter looked hopefully at her. "And we haven't sold a single one yet."

Kathleen looked behind her. "They're failing. They need us."

Emma, Aya, Ethan, and Luke appeared.

"Who are you selling to right now? Or trying to sell to, I should say," Kathleen questioned, walking over to the butterflies.

"I suggested college students, for their parties," Tanner informed her.

Kathleen pursed her lips. "I'll call in my fashion contacts. I'm sure some of them would love something as unique and high-end as this."

The group of friends descended on the room.

"We won't sit back and let you fail. That's not how friends work," Luke assured him as he took a seat

He still struggled with one arm, but he tried to ignore the impact it had on his life. He could shift but he could only hobble, which meant he hadn't been able to run with his pack since the accident. It ate at him, but there was nothing he could do. It would heal at its own pace. There was a lot shifters could do, but performing magic wasn't one of them and this time someone else's potion wasn't going to help.

The team split up into smaller groups, each with a different target in mind. Kathleen tasked Aya to help her talk to the fashion people, while Luke and Peter tried to convince the shifters it would be fantastic for their get-togethers. Tanner, Alison, and Emma worked to pin down college students.

The room was bursting with conversations and increasing happiness, and the sales started to trickle in.

Kathleen fell into the role easily, working the crowd. Alison glanced back at her and marveled once again how Kathleen was so comfortable in her element, laughing at the smooth sales pitch. *They'll never see her coming.*

"Darling, it's so good to hear your voice. I've received the most incredible deal. You need to jump on it right this instant."

"Oh?"

"You know I only bring you the very best. An up and coming entrepreneur—someone you need to keep an eye on—has this wonderful little creation. It's entirely hand-made and unique. You know that's in vogue right now."

"I'm listening."

"Well, those parties you love to host have dwindled a little, haven't they? You need the next big thing to put you on top."

Silence.

"I have the perfect thing. This entrepreneur has created small butterflies, entirely handmade, and imbued them with music magic. They can be tweaked to fill as large or small a space as you need, and because they're magic, no one outside your chosen radius will hear a single note. No more concerns over the noise complaints."

"Butterflies, you say?"

Kathleen grinned, knowing she had him hooked. "Yes. They're made from the very best silk and delicate copper wire. Each one is completely unique. They'll make darling ornaments or broaches once the music magic is depleted. They can be altered to produce whatever music you choose."

"When can he have them available?"

"They can be shipped tomorrow morning if you're able to pay the rush fee."

"You know I'm perfectly able. I'll take six. I'll try them at Friday's party. If I like them, I'll buy more. Should I keep this under wraps or can I tell others?"

Kathleen chewed her bottom lip a second while she assessed which would produce a higher profit margin for Peter.

"Keep them to yourself. It will improve your social standing if they're a secret thing. I'm sure you can find some arrangement with the creator that will suit you both."

"It's always a pleasure to hear from you, Kathleen."

"And you, darling. I'm sure the party will be a hit."

"I sold six." Kathleen looked around at everyone else. "How many have you sold?"

"Four, so we need to sell ten more." Luke jotted down the delivery address.

"No, we sold eight, with the potential for twenty more next week." Tanner passed Peter the addresses.

"We sold another four," Ethan said.

Peter couldn't contain his joy. He hugged Ethan tight. Thanks to his friends, there was a chance. He'd be able to use that money toward college and save a little to continue growing the business. Things just might work out.

"What would I do without you guys?" He grinned at his friends like a fool.

Alison laughed. "Starve and miss half your classes."

Peter started to argue, but she wasn't wrong.

CHAPTER TWENTY-ONE

A lison couldn't sleep. The rain lashed down, hiding the stars. It wasn't suitable weather for walking the grounds, so she decided to slip into the basement to practice her magic. There were things she was still refining.

Pulling on a lightweight hoodie, she stepped into the corridor and ran down the stairs to the basement entrance. A glimmer caught her attention. She hadn't expected anyone to be down there as it was long past lights-out.

Alison crept down the steps and saw Professor Powell in the darkness. Frowning, she inched closer, remaining hidden in the shadows. His power pulsed with dark magic —thick tendrils of oily black with shards of deep blue-black. Alison narrowed her eyes. She had suspected that he was still involved in dark magic. The headmistress trusted him, but something bad was clearly happening around the school. The dead animals had decreased, but they were still present, and no one had found the cause. She wondered if he was working with Professor Heineken.

Professor Powell whispered under his breath, and

Alison watched in horror as the dark magic slithered into the basement. He was practicing again. She'd seen it with her own eyes and needed to tell the headmistress. Alison turned and tried to tip-toe away, but she felt the professor's eyes on her back. A glance over her shoulder showed her that he raced up the stairs toward her. She could either try to run or bind him.

It had never been in Alison's nature to run. She squared her shoulders and summoned her magic. It came quickly and easily, as naturally as breathing. Professor Powell was almost on her when she bound him with thick shadow. A smirk formed on his mouth, and he broke through the bindings without missing a step.

Alison swallowed and prepared to defend herself against a skilled dark magician. To her surprise, Professor Powell stopped and said, "Since you're here, you can help. It doesn't matter that you're a student. Come on."

She frowned and tried to see if this was some form of trap. His soul's colors were anxious, but there was no malice present that she could see. He closed the basement door and looked expectantly at her.

"This isn't what you think." He restrained his impatience.

Alison followed him down the stairs. Xander wiped a hand over his face and tried to collect his thoughts. She was hardly the ally he would have chosen in this fight, but he couldn't allow Robert to escape. He was far too dangerous, and he suspected that he had already hurt people.

The young Drow looked at him with deep suspicion, and he didn't blame her.

"This all started a very long time ago." Xander could remember it as though it was yesterday.

It had also been a dark and stormy night. He and his friends had gathered in a hidden room beneath the local forest. Originally, it had been a root cellar, but they had claimed it as their little sanctuary. Dried herbs and roots hung from the dirt ceiling as one of their group was a talented herb and potion witch. Xander swallowed as he remembered Lynn. She had been such a bright soul in their group, with a smile for everyone and eyes that danced with merriment.

Robert had called the friends together that night. He refused to tell them what it was about until all six were present. The air was thick with nerves and anticipation. Xander had leaned back against the cool wall and waited. Robert was prone to melodrama, and he suspected that this was another instance. The younger man had fought to earn his place within the group. He had found them practicing dark magic and wanted desperately to join their ranks. For a year, he had run errands and done perilous tasks to bring them dangerous objects and spells. Finally, the group had treated him as one of them.

Lynn busied herself separating fresh herbs and tying them into neat little bundles ready to be used. Robert had paced back and forth beneath the slender pair of swords set into the ceiling which had been part of the ritual that bound them together as a group. What they were doing was dangerous and would land them in a lot of trouble if any of them talked. Xander hadn't liked the way Robert kept glancing at the blades. He had worked hard to get out of doing the ritual that would bind him as it had the others.

Though he had finally submitted, Xander had suspected he had tried to find a way around it.

Finally, James arrived, dripping wet with his dark-blond hair plastered to his scalp and his grey eyes as stormy as the night outside.

He strode up to Robert, scowling. "This had better not be another one of your little games, Robert, because I am weary with you and your foolishness."

James had always been the hothead of the group. Robert swallowed hard but maintained eye contact.

"There is a traitor within the group. Someone has siphoned off our power and used it for their own gain."

Xander laughed. No one would do such a ridiculous thing. They had worked as a group to explore the true potential of dark magic. People automatically went to the curses and the destruction, but there was so much more to it than that. They had made some interesting progress on the concept of harnessing chaos as a constructive force. Some of the group had wanted to focus more on exploring the World in Between—the dark and dangerous place where things that should never walk the earth roamed.

Robert spun to glare at Xander.

"You dare laugh at me?"

Xander pushed off the wall. "Why wouldn't I laugh at you? You are the weakest of us, a melodramatic errand boy," he sneered.

"And how much have you told your girlfriend, Mara?" Robert looked around the rest of the group. "Have you broken the oath?"

Xander raised his eyebrow. Mara knew that he dabbled in dark magic, but she had no idea to what extent. She would never understand, and he knew that. It hurt him to have to hide this, but he needed to protect her.

"Get to your point before we remind you what happens to traitors." Xander took a step closer to Robert.

The group whispered around them. Part of the oath they had all taken stated that telling another soul—living or dead—what they did there would result in a bloody and brutal death.

"Lynn." Robert pointed to the startled witch. "She has siphoned the power for herself. You overlook her because she is some innocent herb witch but look closer, Xander. See her true form. She is a malicious—" Sara slapped him.

"How dare you speak such lies!" Sara's magic flared around her hands. "You are jealous that she is better than you in every possible way."

"He is a risk to this group and all we work toward." James stepped closer to Robert. "He can remain here no longer."

The friends closed in around Robert. Xander remembered the feeling of almost predatory anger that flowed through the group that night. A coldness gleamed in James' eyes and the hurt on Lynn's face was painful to witness.

Robert's face contorted into something monstrous. "I have proof. Look at my evidence, and you'll understand."

Looks passed between the group members. Robert had always been something of an outsider, never fitting in. If they were honest with themselves, they had used him as their errand boy and some light entertainment. They had never meant for him to be one of them. Not really.

"You are lying." Sara pressed into Robert's space. "Lynn is the heart and kindness of this group."

Xander looked away from Alison. "It all happened so fast."

No one had felt Robert's magic forming around him. When they had looked afterward, they found a small artifact, a shard of bone imbued with magic so dark even they wouldn't touch it. He had glared at Lynn, his body tense with pure fury. His hands clenched into fists, and the next thing Xander knew, Lynn's body went limp and she crumpled to the floor. James and Sara leapt on Robert and beat him to the ground. They bound him with magic while Xander and Elise ran to their friend.

She looked eternally surprised, her eyes wide open and her mouth in a neat 'O.' Xander couldn't find a pulse, and her body was already cooling. There wasn't a single thread of life left in her. It should have taken a few minutes for her magic and life to leave her body, but it was as though it had dissipated in a puff of smoke.

Elise moved Lynn's body to the ratty old armchair in the corner and closed her eyes. She wrapped her shoulders in her favorite plum-colored shawl, and for a moment, she looked almost like she was sleeping. James hauled Robert to his feet. Xander, as the unofficial leader, walked up to him.

"He tore the life out of her." Xander fought to control his anger. "He must suffer a fate worse than death."

Sara looked at him with a cold, calculating expression.

"You think we should strip his magic?"

"Yes."

Xander looked back to that moment. He had told himself that he wasn't a killer, that he was better than that. Now, he realized he should have taken Robert's life. At the time, it had seemed fitting to make the man suffer a life without the thing he adored and craved more than anything. It had been poetic, in a way, but he had since learned that poetic punishment often led to far more darkness and pain in the future. It was better to remove all chance of retribution.

Robert thrashed and screamed, but Sara gagged him with dark tendrils of magic. They had tied him down to stakes driven into the damp floor. His eyes went wide, and he swung between muffled entreaties and fury that they would dare to do this to him. His words were garbled, but the intent was painted as plain as day on his face.

Alison was fascinated by his story. She had never seen Professor Powell speak with such raw honesty before. Everyone knew that he had darkness in his past, but she had never pictured anything quite like this.

"As the leader, it was my job to remove his magic. The others were all involved, of course, but it was my hand that wrenched it from his body."

Sara had fought back the tears, making her eyes glisten while Elise and James wore masks of pure fury. This was not a ritual they had performed before, but they had each read up on it. A few months earlier, they'd discussed it because they walked a dangerous path and their enemies would become increasingly ruthless. They had made sure to focus their studies on magic that could be used to defend and disable enemies.

James shuddered as he placed the final crystal on Robert's chest, right over his heart. To lose your magic was to lose a large part of who and what you were. They would strip away his life's purpose.

Xander glanced back at Lynn and hardened his resolve. The man had taken her life without reason other than some insane theory that only existed in his mind. Xander formed a dagger from pure dark magic. The rest of the group stood at the four points of the compass and whispered the required spell.

Their prisoner thrashed with everything he had as he felt his magic dragged to the surface. Xander cut a neat line from Robert's heart to his belly button. He felt the man's magic slip out of his body into the surrounding darkness. Xander ignored the feeling of guilt and quiet regret in his mind and focused on carving the four symbols required to pull the deepest of the magic out into the ether.

Robert stilled entirely when Xander carved the final line. He stood over him, sent the dagger back to the ether, and raised his arms to the sky above. He felt Robert's magic evaporating around them as Xander called upon the final piece of dark enchantment. He looked into Robert's eyes as he drove the dark power deep into him and pulled out the final spark.

It was done.

Xander allowed James and Sara to deal with Robert while he went to Lynn and performed a quiet ritual to make sure her spirit was well received. In his periphery, he was aware of Robert shoved out into the dark night.

Sara brought a small white stone to him. It carried an odd aura.

Xander peered at it and frowned. "Is that a fairy bone or a piece of a rib, maybe?"

She handed it to him, and he held it up to the magical white orb. The light rippled over it, and he saw the tiny carvings in the bones. There had been rumors that someone had slaughtered a fairy and taken their bones. The group had limits. They had sworn never to touch blood or bone magic. Both were beyond where they were willing to tread.

Yet Robert had a piece of fairy bone, which told Xander he had already gone far beyond the group's limits. It had sent a chill down him, and the group had destroyed the small artifact. Some things should never exist.

"What do we tell Lynn's family?" Sara wiped furiously at her eyes. "We can't tell them the truth."

Xander summoned his inner strength. "We tell them she was attacked by a dark wizard. She died valiantly, protecting her friends."

"And what about Robert?" James shoved his hands into his pockets. "He's still out there."

"He is useless without his magic. He is no concern of ours anymore," Xander said.

He squeezed his eyes closed and rubbed his temples. He couldn't have imagined how wrong he had been with those words. Robert had been far more intelligent and determined than any of them had given him any credit for.

He looked at Alison before continuing with his story.

"He went after Mara first, not that she knew it."

They had been madly in love. Mara had loved dating the bad boy with a heart of gold, and Xander adored her passion for life. Six months had passed since the incident with Robert and the group hadn't returned to that room since. No one had dared mentioned Robert or Lynn's names.

"I don't know how he did it, but somehow, Robert

managed to find some truly dark magic to wield as his own. He became something twisted and warped, no longer a person as you think of them. We had been out camping as a group. Mara was with us, as was Sara's boyfriend, Aaron.

"The campfire died without warning, and a thick curtain of darkness descended over us. We knew it was dark magic. Robert's voice cut through the darkness as James and I tore the curtain apart. His body looked like an experiment from a horror novel."

Xander sighed.

"We didn't have a choice. We couldn't defend ourselves with light magic. It wouldn't have touched a monster like him. Mara never understood that, but we couldn't break the oath and tell her what had happened with Robert. He had always liked Mara, and the way he leered at her brought out murderous impulses in me. Perhaps I should have indulged them on that night given that I lost Mara anyway.

"Once his little curtain of darkness had been torn aside, Robert made a small speech or tried to. Sara cut him off before he could say anything that would make our loved ones ask too many questions. Mara asked, of course, but she didn't have enough information to make me break the oath.

"Robert went after Aaron who was a skilled witch, but he never stood a chance. Aaron had sat near the fire, confused, while the rest of us tried to drive Robert off. Somehow, he managed to sneak around behind Sara and Elise, and all I heard was the gurgle. His final breath before he—"

Xander looked at Alison and decided she was too young to hear such horrific details.

"We used dark magic to drive Robert off. We couldn't remove his stolen magic, and we couldn't break through his defenses to kill him. Our only option was to drive him off and hope he didn't return for us again.

"Only he did return. Elise was killed next. She was found at the center of a ritual sacrifice. Her beautiful face was forever frozen in an expression of agony and fear.

"James suffered a little less, or so we think. We can't be entirely sure since we only found some parts of his body, barely enough to know that he died.

"I'm the only one left of that group. If I don't kill him this time, he will hunt Mara down. I am reasonably certain he was the one who hurt your shifter friend. He always despised shifters and felt they were nothing more than mutts to be used. There were multiple occasions where he tried to convince us to make artifacts from shifters. We refused, of course. We weren't monsters.

"Still, there have been several shifter murders over the years that I am reasonably certain were his handiwork."

Alison glared at him. "Brownstone would have been able to use that information." The fact that he had chosen to hide that knowledge to save his own ass irritated her.

"I'm not positive that the murders were done by him, and how would I explain it to your father or another authority?" He looked at Alison. "As you are aware, the best thing we can do sometimes is remain quiet."

Alison refused to look away from him as she wondered if he knew about the darkness that had escaped the pendant. Was she responsible for more deaths because she never found out what the darkness was and defeated it?

"Robert is nearby, and he must be stopped. We cannot allow him to continue killing people, Alison. You cannot tell anyone else about this. Do you understand? We cannot pull more people into this."

Alison thought it through. She didn't agree with his methods, but she could at least understand his reasoning. She hadn't told anyone about the darkness from the pendant yet. Was this really so different?

CHAPTER TWENTY-TWO

As she ate her oatmeal, Alison mulled over what Professor Powell had told her the night before. She was responsible for whatever the darkness from the pendant did, just as the professor was at least partially responsible for Robert's actions. The sun was shining, and the grounds looked as though they had dried out. It was the perfect time to investigate what had really happened to the dead animals.

Her friends were all still in bed, enjoying the relaxation the weekend provided. She headed out toward the woods where most of the animals had been found. Everything was deceptively peaceful and quiet. The remaining birds chirped from the woods, and Dorvu enjoyed a nap in a sunny spot in the middle of a field. Alison spotted a lone rabbit in the distance. The dragon would be happy that at least some were left.

She had tucked her glasses in her pocket so that she could focus on her magical sight. The woods appeared as they usually did with threads of magic buried deep within the tree trunks and branches. Small spots of life energy skittered through the trees overhead. They were likely the squirrels and small songbirds.

After an hour of walking around the woods, including the area where the fight with the rogue had occurred, she had to admit that everything looked as it always had. That meant that she needed one or two of the bodies to look at, which would entail an awkward conversation with Horace.

She knew it wouldn't be easy, but she couldn't let things continue as they were. This was her responsibility after all.

Horace sat on the bench near the barn with his eyes closed, enjoying the sun on his face. Alison felt bad disturbing his rare moment of quiet, but there was no time like the present.

"Horace?"

She approached the bench and waited.

The groundskeeper's energy shifted, and he focused on her.

"And what can I do for you this morning?"

"I wanted to look at the dead animals if I could. I might be able to give us some insight into what happened to them."

His mouth thinned a little.

"You're usually so open and honest with your friends and me. Why don't you tell me the whole story?"

Alison had been caught off guard. Did Horace know about the pendant?

"Well, I want to be a bounty hunter like my dad. This seemed like a good place to start."

Suspicion threaded through Horace, but he didn't say anything more.

"I'm afraid I destroyed all the recent bodies last night, and I didn't find any this morning."

She tried not to let her disappointment show.

"You should really talk to your friends, though. Secrets have destroyed many a good relationship."

Alison raised an eyebrow. He must know what had happened with the pendant. She didn't know how, but he was right. She needed to confide the truth about the darkness that had emerged from it. They deserved to know and might be able to help her figure out what it was. She'd looked through the library, but there weren't many books on secret and possibly illegal magical pendant creation.

She smiled. "Thanks, Horace. Although you might want to work on your subtlety."

He laughed, and she headed back to the school building. There was no time like the present.

Alison waited impatiently as her friends ate their breakfast. Conversation was sparse as they had stayed up a lot later than usual studying. Finals were taking it out of everyone. Once they had eaten, she ushered them into a quiet corner of the library, away from the other students who were cramming.

She looked at them, then away. "I have something I need to tell you. It's about the night with the rogue and the pendant."

"We killed him," Kathleen hissed.

Alison held up her hand. "It's about the pendant. It wasn't quite as straightforward as it looked. A darkness emerged when it was created. I thought it was simply weird residual magic at first, but I think I saw the darkness at the train station when I headed home for Christmas. Then, the animals started dying this semester, and I think maybe that darkness is responsible for it. I don't know what it is. My best guess is that it's something death-related to balance the life the pendant gave. I haven't been able to find anything out about it in the…well, in here." She pointed to the books around them.

Emma leaned a little closer. "Why did you wait months to tell us? What the hell, Alison? We're supposed to be your best friends."

"I wasn't sure what it was. I didn't want to worry you over nothing," Alison admitted with a shrug.

"Those animals started dying right after Christmas." Peter glared at her. "You should have told us then."

Kathleen crossed her arms. "You know you're really arrogant sometimes. You think you're better than us. You have your bounty hunter dad and your Drow magic, so you think you have to protect us because we're inferior."

"It's not like that." Alison reached out to her. "It's not."

Kathleen pulled away.

"Really, Alison? It's not? Come on. You're always so smug when you help someone out in class with your special magic. The rest of us screw up sometimes, but no, not Alison Brownstone. So, you thought you could do this alone and be some special bounty hunter." Kathleen stood up. "Well, I'm out. You wanted to be on your own. You got it."

Tanner sighed. "You really should have told us, Alison."

She didn't need her natural vision to see the hurt in him. It was written all over his face.

"I'm with Kathleen. This was a really dick move, Alison. Look, I get it, you're special. But we're supposed to be in this together. We do these things together. I assume you want some help now. So we're finally of some use to you." Emma scowled.

Alison tried to hold her temper in check.

"There hasn't been the right moment. It's not an easy topic to broach."

"We talked about the dead animals at least once a day when it first happened." Emma threw up her hands. "How about one of those times?"

Alison didn't have an answer for that. Emma was right, and she knew it.

"I'm sorry, okay. I screwed up."

Tanner squeezed her hand. "So, what do you know? Anything useful?"

She took a moment to calm herself. "Not really. It's all speculation. It doesn't seem to go too far from the school, though, which is something."

Ira could feel the darkness closing on him. He still wasn't sure what exactly it was, but he knew that time was running out. It edged closer, and the pure, impenetrable blackness consumed his dreams. He couldn't remember the last time he had felt like himself or had a good night's sleep. It ate away at him, piece by piece.

His ritual room was a chaotic mess. He had painted

fresh runes and symbols on the walls again and again, trying to boost his own magic while also protecting himself. He was out of the kemana crystal's magic now, and his own power was slipping between his fingertips. No matter what he tried, he couldn't make things align as he needed. The darkness consumed his mind, making it difficult to focus. He looked at the runes and frowned. He had known what they did when he painted them, but now, they were nothing more than brightly painted lines.

The darkness was almost a physical presence in the back of his mind. It made the hairs on the back of his neck stand on end. He no longer felt safe leaving his cottage at night. Ira laughed, a harsh, bitter sound as he looked around his small cottage. What had once felt like a home now felt like a comfortable cage, and it had been all his own doing. Yet he still felt no regret. Perhaps the darkness had taken that, too. He had worked to improve the world, to create a state which would allow magical people to access their full potential. They were so limited by their natural-given magic.

The Brotherhood had officially disowned him two days ago. He was on his own. There was no one who could possibly help him now. He had tried telling them about the darkness, but they assumed his mind was fading. They hadn't believed a word and claimed he'd brought shame upon them. After everything he had done in their name, the final betrayal had hurt the most.

If he could find out what the darkness was and reach the magic at the heart of the crystal, he could fix everything. He was sure of it. Jason Parker was everywhere he turned, though. For a moment, he wondered if perhaps

Jason was the darkness. No, he was merely a student. Ira had looked through the private library—the professor's library—but he hadn't been able to find anything there. Focus was too difficult, leaving him unable to grasp topics he should have understood.

His thoughts were erratic, and he struggled to maintain a facade that the professors and students wouldn't question. Ira used every spare penny of his money on potions to soothe his mind and feed small boosts to his remaining magic, barely enough that he could continue to teach. He had made the students do most of the work and called it practice.

No one had questioned his methods yet, but they would. Time was slipping away as quickly as his magic. He wasn't sure which one would vanish first, but he knew that he only had one last chance. It was risky, but what choice did he have?

CHAPTER TWENTY-THREE

Alison was making her way to the barn when Christie rushed up to her.

"Hi. I saw you out the window. Do you normally wander around at night by yourself? It's very safe here, isn't it? It's not like London which really isn't very safe after dark. I mean, some areas are okay, but some are really dangerous. We have magic, but you have to be careful how you use it. What are you doing? How are finals going? Are you excited to go to college?"

Alison took a moment to run through everything the younger girl had said. There were way too many words and questions in there.

"I'm taking a nice walk on a beautiful night. I planned to do some star-gazing. My friend gave me a telescope." Alison ran her fingers over the small device.

She could feel Izzie's relaxed happiness, and her frustration at being disturbed by Christie faded away.

"Oh, that's so cool. Are senior finals really scary? I don't like exams. I mean, I get good grades, but they're so stress-

195

ful. You have no idea what to study, which I get is the point, but I always panic a little and study too much. Then I don't get any sleep. I think I keep the concealer company in business."

Alison laughed. Christie had so much energy, and in a way, she envied her that.

"Senior finals are difficult, but if you're getting good grades, I'm sure you won't have any problems when you get there. I'm hoping to go to Georgetown." Alison looked up at the stars. "Do you know what you want to do yet?"

"I'm not sure. I'm torn between archaeology and politics. I want to help people, but I'm not sure how I want to do it yet. I mean, archaeology doesn't sound like it can help people, but if we can get a better understanding of our past, I think we can encourage and grow a more positive future. Georgetown's a good school, right? I don't really know American schools. Your mum's an archaeologist, right? Isn't she one of those really cool adventure ones?"

Alison laughed at the image of Shay's face if she knew she was called a cool adventure archaeologist.

"Yeah, my mom retrieves rare and ancient artifacts. She seems to enjoy it, but it's not as easy as it looks, though. It can be a very difficult job."

"Oh, I know. I'm getting fitter, and I'm studying all sorts of different history and how to handle dangerous artifacts. Some of them contain ancient, deadly magic. I'm not sure if that's what I want to do or not. The idea of adventure is really appealing, but I don't know how much risk and danger I want in my life. Then again, politics isn't necessarily always safe, especially with the attitude some magicals have toward the human government. I think we can work on that. No one's perfect, and we're kind of scary to them. I mean have you seen what we can do with magic?"

Alison wasn't really in the mood for a political debate, but she let Christie run on.

"I can see the human perspective, but I agree that things do need to be better balanced."

"Oh yes, balance is very important. People get so extreme, and they get scared which only makes them more extreme. Georgetown is a good school, isn't it? You need good grades to get in, right? But it's one that looks amazing on your C.V., so you can get whatever job you want. Do you need a C.V. to be a bounty hunter? How do you get into that? I mean, can anyone do it? Is there a license?"

"What's a C.V?" Alison scrunched up her nose.

"You know, where you list everything you know and can do. You give it to the company you are trying to work for."

Alison smiled. "Oh, we call it a resume here. Yes, Georgetown is a very good school. No, you don't need a... C.V. to be a bounty hunter, but I'd like a degree as a backup. I'll study criminal psychology, which will be very useful."

"You must be so excited. College is a huge deal. It's when you get some independence, but I mean, we kind of have independence here. We live away from our parents, at least, and the professors aren't too strict. The kitchen pixies can be a bit scary sometimes, though. Criminal psychology sounds fascinating and quite scary. I mean, I don't know if I want to get into the heads of some of those criminals. The things they do are really depraved. It might give you nightmares. I've heard that the people who truly understand those types of people are a little different. They must be. Not that I think you're weird or anything. You're always so nice and perfectly normal."

Alison sat down on the grass. "I am pretty excited. It's a big change. And thanks, I think. It's nice to know that I'm reasonably normal. I'm looking forward to criminal psychology. I think the differences in how they view and interact with the world is fascinating."

"You're friends with Luke, the shifter who got hurt in the Louper game, right? How's he doing? Do you know who or what did it? He must be devastated. It's must be hard for shifters to not be able to run. And he's a really good Louper player, too. His team must be heartbroken. We were doing great too."

Alison smiled. "Luke is doing okay. He's healing slower than he would like, and he's upset he can't run with his pack. He's still training with the Louper team, and they're confident they'll do well in their next match."

Alison knew that Luke wasn't doing okay at all. He felt like he was caged, and she had found him hobbling through the woods in his wolf form a few times. He'd said that he needed to be on four legs sometimes, for his sanity. His pack had been understanding, but it was hard on him.

"We're not sure who hurt him. We suspect it was the rival team going too far."

Alison hated lying to Christie, but she couldn't tell her the truth. Professor Powell's old friend had likely injured Luke in some twisted blow against the professor or because Luke was a shifter. She wasn't sure but did, however, know that Robert would pay for everything he had done.

"The next Louper match is the final in the championship, right? That's so exciting. I never saw any before I came here. They're so thrilling. I'm still sorry for the game I interrupted last semester, though. I thought about trying to join the team, but I'm not sure if it's right for me. I mean, there's so much running around, and while it's fun exploring new places, they can be risky too. I think I'm better off cheering the team on."

"Yes, the next match is the final in the championship. We're confident that the team has what it takes to win. And no, playing Louper never really appealed to me either."

Something changed in the magic around the telescope, and Alison laid down on the grass and put it to her eye. She knew that Izzie lay somewhere looking at the same stars. Alison couldn't keep the smile from her face. It felt as though her best friend was right beside her. She gazed up at the pinpoints of light against the black fabric of the sky and allowed all other thoughts and feelings to slip away.

For that short time, she was back with Izzie once again, and everything was okay. Christie had lain down next to Alison and looked up at the stars with wide eyes and a gentle smile. Alison didn't think she'd ever seen the girl so quiet and peaceful before.

The soft flapping of Dorvu's wings caught Alison's attention, and she slipped away, trying not to disturb Christie. Horace sat at his fire with his scruffy dog near his feet.

The groundskeeper smiled at her. "How're you feeling today? You look much calmer."

"I shared the secret. It didn't go smoothly, but it's

shared now, at least," Alison confessed, looking for the dragon.

"Dorvu's been waiting for you." Horace nodded toward the incoming creature. "He thought you'd forgotten."

The silver dragon swooped down and landed with a slight stumble. The grin on his face was clear for all to see.

"Did you bring your skates like I asked you, too?" He fixed her with an intent look. "You did remember, right?"

Alison held up her ice-skates.

"How could I forget?"

The dragon's grin widened before he walked a short distance from the fire and blew on the grass. A thin layer of white ice covered the ground. He continued blowing more frosty air until a thick layer of ice formed. Alison put her skates on and laughed with unrepentant glee as she skated around the small rink Dorvu created for her. The dragon circled slowly around the space, blowing more frosty air over it to make sure it didn't melt.

A quiet sadness settled into Alison's stomach as she realized this would be the last time she could skate on one of Dorvu's rinks. It was already late in spring, and there wasn't much left of the school year now. She glided to the dragon and wrapped her arms around his great neck. She wasn't one for big displays of affection, but she would miss him and his gentle nature.

"Don't be sad. We have lots of good memories." He nudged her. "Skate. I want to see your new moves."

Alison laughed and attempted some fancy spins. She fell over twice, which delighted Dorvu even more. When she grew tired, the dragon allowed the rink to melt and Alison removed her skates. She focused on all the happy memories they'd created and tried to ignore the fact that their time together was coming to an end.

Christie had joined Horace by the fire, and Alison settled down near the flames to warm up.

"Do you have any idea who hurt Luke in the Louper game?" Christie looked at Horace. "Is it normal for teams to go that far?"

The groundskeeper looked at Alison. She knew that he knew all the goings on at the school and wouldn't be surprised if he had witnessed Professor Powell telling his story.

"No, it's not normal. There are strict rules in place, but there will always be those who take things too far." He frowned. "There are always people who are never satisfied with what they have been given in life. They push to have more and more until suddenly, they have nothing at all."

Alison frowned. She had the distinct sense that the groundskeeper wasn't talking about Luke's injury anymore. There must have been something else there. It could have been Robert and his quest for dark magic, but she suspected it was another person.

"I believe it's time for you girls to get to bed." Horace stood. "Good night."

Alison wouldn't let things go quite that easily. She intended to keep digging the following morning into everything that had happened to find out exactly what she had missed.

CHAPTER TWENTY-FOUR

Alison picked at her breakfast. She wasn't in the mood for any of it, and her stomach was full of butterflies. Word had spread around the school that the first of the college acceptance letters had come through. For the first time in months, breakfast was quiet. The students were subdued as they waited for their mail. The kitchen pixies had prepared French toast as a treat to try and cheer the students up. Finding out which college you had or hadn't gotten into always made for a tumultuous morning.

Kathleen put on a brave face, but Alison saw the nervous energy running through her. She was as worried as everyone else. Peter occupied himself by reading some journal article on an advancement between magic and technology. Ethan fidgeted constantly and couldn't sit still. Alison herself was quietly confident, but she couldn't hide the slight nervousness. She hoped to get into Georgetown —not an easy feat with all the competition out there—and worried that she might not have enough extracurriculars on her application.

"Would you stop." Aya glared at Ethan. "Be still."

Ethan ignored her. He'd worked hard to make it to college, and this was a huge day for them all. Too much nervous energy meant he was unable to stay still. He would pace if he thought the kitchen pixies would allow it.

After what felt like forever, the mail was brought around to the various tables. The pixies had magicked away all food and drinks to reduce the mess should some students not get their desired placements. They learned that lesson the hard way. In the past, some of the more hot-blooded students had thrown drinks and food when they had been disappointed.

Each of the friends looked down at their letters. Inside was the moment of truth, the plans for their future. Alison went first. She tore her letter open and skimmed it, looking for the keyword 'accepted.' There it was. She read through the letter twice, word by word, before she allowed herself to react.

"I'm in. I'm going to Georgetown to major in criminal psychology."

Tanner put his arm around her shoulders and kissed her cheek.

"I'm so proud of you."

Alison saw his pride shining through. It would have been easy for him to be slightly bitter over her determination to follow in her father's footsteps, but there wasn't a trace. He was a good guy, and she felt happy to have him at her side.

Peter let out a whoop of joy. "I have an internship at the

New York Times. The managing director is an elf, so I should be able to cover some stories that intersect the human and magical communities. Dude, do you have any idea how freakin' amazing this is? The New York Times. This isn't a small newspaper and could help me form connections and set me up for the most amazing career."

He sat and looked at his second letter. "And I'm going to NYU. I'm in their journalism course. I can't believe this is really happening. Someone pinch me."

Tanner and Ethan both reached across and pinched him with a laugh.

Peter's grin widened to rival the Cheshire Cat's. "I'm not dreaming. And we made more than enough from selling the butterflies that my share gives me enough to get started."

"Congratulations!"

"You'll rock it."

Tanner smiled at his friend. "The world needs good journalists like you. We're all really proud of you."

"What about you guys?" Peter looked around. "Did you get in?"

Kathleen waved her letter. "Of course I did. I am going to Parsons School of Design where I will begin my path as the next fashionista. You can expect to see my lines walking down the catwalks in a couple of years. I plan to be a household name within a decade. Of course, I won't do high-street fashion. I only deal with high society. I might invite you to some of my parties, assuming you're still worthy, that is."

Emma rolled her eyes and muttered, "You're designing clothes, not becoming royalty."

Kathleen's scowl was forgotten when Tanner shared his news.

"I'm in too. I got onto the medical program at George-town." He hugged Alison tightly. "We'll be close. I can't believe I actually pulled it off."

She wrapped her arms around him and rested her cheek against his. Everything was going according to plan. She'd been worried that she'd lose Tanner. He'd become her anchor. Now that they would both be at branches of Georgetown, they'd have a couple more years together and time to figure everything else out.

Aya looked at him. "Do you know which field you want to go into—with medicine, I mean?"

"Pediatrics with a focus on the magical community." Tanner kissed Alison's cheek. "I want to make a difference, and I feel like I can best do that with kids."

Kathleen pulled a faux-disgusted expression. "Ugh, you guys are sickeningly sweet, all helping the world be better, mending sick kids, and catching criminals. You make the rest of us look really bad, you know that, right?"

Everyone laughed.

They had all been accepted into their dream school, and the mood couldn't have been any brighter. They went to find Luke who had chosen not to be there when they received their letters. He wasn't sure he would go to college.

Tanner knocked and opened the door to see him in his wolf form with his head resting on his good leg. His ears were low, and he looked utterly miserable.

"Hey, we got into our colleges." Tanner sat on the bed. "Do you want to talk? Maybe we can cheer you up."

The girls hung back in the hallway. They weren't technically supposed to be that close to the guys' dorms, but they wanted to see Luke.

He shifted back into his human form and gave Tanner a small smile before he put his arm back in its sling.

"Congrats. You guys work really hard, and you all deserve it."

Tanner frowned. "Do you know what you're planning to do yet? Can your pack help at all?"

"I think I'll head home for a while to let my arm heal and then I'll see where I stand. I need to tell the team I can't do the Louper match."

"We haven't tried everything yet." Alison walked into the room. "We can try my magic."

Luke looked up at her, a spark of hope shining in his eyes. She smiled. "I don't know if it'll work. I also don't know much about shifter physiology, but we can try."

Everyone crowded into the dorm room and closed the door so no one would see Alison use her power.

She sat beside Luke on his bed and called her magic. Starting with a support system made the most sense. Luke held his arm out and flinched as he felt the cool ribbons of Alison's magic wrap his delicate arm. He flexed his fingers and whined with pain.

"No go. It hurts almost as much with the magic as it does without."

Alison examined his arm and wondered if perhaps something closer to a splint would be a better idea. She adjusted and formed it into a pair of splints, one on either side of the limb. He frowned and shifted into his wolf form. Slowly, he put a little pressure on his injured paw before he yelped and yanked it up.

When he returned to his human form, he held up his good hand.

"Look, I appreciate that you're trying, but I'm not some excuse for you to practice your magic. Thanks, but no thanks." Luke looked for his shoes. "I'm going to talk to the Louper team. See you at lunch."

Luke wasn't looking forward to that conversation with his team. He'd put it off, hoping to find some way to make his wrist heal quicker, but nothing had materialized. They waited for him at the Louper field. He walked with his head low and a dour expression on his face.

"Look, guys, I'm sorry, but I can't play in the next match. I'm useless to you with only one arm."

Etienne crossed his arms. "No. You are not going to back out because of a small injury."

Luke looked at the elf who glared in response.

"I'm with Etienne. You're our captain, and we need you." Cody echoed the defiant pose. "You can't abandon us. This is the championship."

Matt walked up to add his opinion. "Just because you can't shift doesn't make you useless. There's more to us than our wolf forms."

"I can't climb, and I don't know how well I can fight," Luke protested.

"You can lead us. You can run, and you can help us figure out the puzzles." Daniel drew himself a little taller. "You're still our captain. We're a team and we'll win this as a team."

"I won't allow you to skulk away from your last chance

to win this trophy." Etienne gestured at Luke's arm. "That is a small injury. I might forgive your attempt to bow out if it were your ankle and it slowed you down, but it doesn't. So, what will we focus our training on today?"

Luke looked at his teammates and found himself overwhelmed. They each offered him admiration and strength. They had been new players with low stamina and a lack of cohesion when they'd started, and now, they felt like a pack. It would never be the same as running with his fellow wolves, but it was as close as he'd felt since his injury.

"While I don't appreciate the attitude, I do appreciate where it's coming from. You're right. We'll go into this final game with the goal to win the championship. You've worked hard, and you deserve to take that trophy." Luke smiled his first genuine smile in a while. "Today, you'll start with suicide runs. We need to improve that stamina."

The wizards groaned but couldn't keep the smiles off their faces. They finally had their captain back.

Matt patted Luke's shoulder. He understood better than anyone the pain he suffered and couldn't imagine what it felt like to not be able to run.

The shifter smiled. "We'll make you proud, captain."

CHAPTER TWENTY-FIVE

Aya competed with Alison for the mirror. Kathleen had claimed the largest one and now tried to edge over to the second. They were dressing for the spring dance—the last dance they'd attend at the school.

Alison had bought a simple, elegant gown in a pale, silvery-blue with a fitted bustier and a skirt that flared gently to the ground. A small flower-pattern overlay on the left side added a little interest. She'd pinned her hair up into an elaborate up-do.

Kathleen had chosen the opposite, a tight black dress with a plunging neckline and a slit almost to her hip. Her very expensive heels were five inches high, and she leaned closer to the mirror, whispering the spell to apply high-end make-up. Her face slowly became a masterpiece as pitch-black eyeliner was evenly applied to emphasize her eyes along with the false lashes and bold yellow eyeshadow. She ignored the rule that said red lipstick should be worn with simple eye makeup, and her lips became a bold cherry red.

Aya fastened a simple silver necklace with a feather

charm around Alison's neck, one Tanner had given her for one of their anniversaries. She didn't wear it often, but she wanted it on that night.

Emma and Aya had chosen stunning gowns in shades of pink and lilac. The dresses hugged their figures without being quite as flashy as Kathleen's. Aya finished her outfit with a pair of small pins in her hair which she wore in loose curls. Emma's butterfly earrings fluttered gently. Alison thought the movement would irritate her if she wore them, but they worked for her friend.

The guys arrived in black suits complete with black ties, aside from Ethan who wore a bright blue one. No one had been able to convince him to go with black, so they let him be.

Tanner took Alison's hands. "You look stunning. You're an absolute vision."

"You look pretty good yourself." Alison smiled and wrapped her arms around his neck. "We should make tonight count."

"I've already had a word with the club to play our song," he whispered in her ear.

She leaned against him for a moment, enjoying his presence. He always knew the perfect sweet gesture to make their time together really special.

Luke hadn't planned on going to the dance, but his friends hassled him until he finally relented and donned his suit. His arm had healed enough to be without a sling, but it had to remain bound. It was a constant reminder of his weakness and that he couldn't run with his pack. They always took a longer, more joyous run after the dances to burn off the excess energy.

The shifter pushed those thoughts aside and focused on his friends. He wasn't alone in the world, and the dance would be fun. Aya and Kathleen had relaxed around him a little, and Luke suspected that Alison had stepped in and had stern words with them. Still, he walked with Peter and Ethan at the back of the group.

Everyone had put in extra effort for the occasion. The decorations were living plants and flowers that covered the walls with tendrils of bright green and red vines. Flowers of every shape, size, and color hung from the ceiling and sprouted from the creepers and small shrubs. The air was filled with the scents of fresh spring water, honeysuckle, and roses. Luke breathed in deep and smiled.

Gentle music filled the air with a very high-society feel, or so he thought. There wasn't a band, since Peter and his entrepreneurs' club had adapted their butterflies specifically for the night. String quartets played familiar songs that gradually built in tempo, encouraging more students to move out onto the dance floor.

Alison and Tanner danced with large smiles on their faces as the music washed over them. She thought the string covers of the songs was a nice touch. It somehow added to the spring feel of everything. The professors stood at the edge of the room, smiling and laughing. Everything felt relaxed and happy. It was a welcome break from the exams and all the stress they had caused. Once the song ended, they walked hand-in-hand off the dancefloor.

Tanner handed Alison a cup of bright red punch. She took a sip, and her mouth exploded with sour cherry, fresh apple, and a touch of elderflower.

"That's really good." She took another sip. "They should make this available under normal circumstances."

Tanner took a large gulp. "Damn, that *is* good. Maybe we can get the recipe from someone."

"Professor Fowler will probably know. This seems like her kind of thing," Alison mused, looking for magic.

"Are you seriously analyzing the punch?" Ethan crossed his arms. "It's a dance. You're supposed to have fun, not analyze stuff."

Alison laughed. "I can't help myself."

Ethan took them both by the arm and started to drag them away. "Try harder."

The music shifted to something upbeat. He led them onto the dance floor where he proceeded to move to a beat that only he could hear. Tanner and Alison laughed and joined him.

Kathleen had attached herself to a particularly handsome wood elf. She told him her plans to take over the fashion world while he smiled politely, and she danced to the music in the center of the room, making sure everyone could see her. The dress had been her own creation. She had woven a good deal of magic into it, and she felt it was a waste if even a few didn't see her art.

Peter couldn't quite relax. He kept a close eye on the butterflies hidden amongst the flowers. A little voice in the back of his mind reminded him of the issues they'd had the first time the butterflies were used together. They'd sold over a hundred since then and not had a single complaint. These were his friends, though, so it was different.

Finally, Luke grabbed Peter and marched him onto the floor where a pretty witch waited to dance with him.

"You're welcome," the shifter whispered before he disappeared into the crowd.

Luke's pack instincts had kicked in strongly. He moved through the crowd, making sure all his friends were happy and had what they needed. Perversely, he couldn't stay still and he couldn't relax enough to dance. His pack was out there, and they'd be ready for their run soon.

Alison hooked her arm through Luke's good one and pulled him back into the chaos.

"Relax and dance," she ordered him.

"It's really hard to relax on command, but I can try." He smiled.

Their favorite song came on, and they threw their hands up, releasing all inhibitions as they embraced the music and sang along. Laughter filled the air, and for those few minutes, Luke forgot all his woes and allowed himself to be happy.

The dance concluded with Tanner and Alison's song. They slow-danced with contented expressions on their faces. She rested her head on his shoulder and closed her eyes, feeling safe in his arms. Hopefully, she could look forward to many more moments like this with him. Bounty hunting wouldn't make a life with him easy, but the more time she spent with Tanner, the more determined she was to make it work. She couldn't imagine anyone else making her heart flutter the way he did.

The dance had finished an hour before and everyone changed back into their casual clothes, not wanting to ruin expensive gowns and suits. They hung out at the bottom of the staircase, talking.

"What do you think my chances are of getting the apple pie recipe from the pixies before we go?" Ethan looked in the direction of the kitchen. "Maybe if I flatter them..."

Tanner chuckled and squeezed Ethan's shoulder. "You don't have a chance. They'll take those recipes to their graves. You'll have to accept a life with second-class apple pie."

Ethan's hands shot to his heart, and he adopted an exaggerated expression of horror. "No! How can I possibly go on?" He keeled backward onto the stairs. "A world with subpar apple pie is a dark world indeed."

"You should have gone to acting school." Alison nudged his thigh with her toe. "With those skills, you'll be famous in no time."

"I want to give everyone else a chance. It's not fair if I do everything." Ethan grinned.

Luke froze. He heard the pained and panicked cries of his pack. His heart thudded in his chest, and he stood, looking alarmed. He needed to get to them, but he couldn't run.

"Luke?" Alison reached for his good arm.

"My pack. They're under attack. I need to get to them."

Ethan sprang to his feet. "Follow me. I can liberate the car."

They bolted out into the darkness after Ethan. The night felt like it was closing in around Luke as he heard his pack again. He needed to be there. Ethan dropped to his knees with his lockpick set, making quick work of the locks on the workshop. He thrust the door open and ran inside with Luke hot on his heels. The shifter dove into the passenger seat as Ethan started the car. Everyone else piled into the back.

No one needed to say a word. They couldn't stand by while the pack was in trouble. The tires screeched on the concrete as Ethan accelerated onto the school grounds. He raced across the grass and took a shortcut through the woods. Branches and shrubs scraped the vehicle and sounded like claws against the glass windows.

The vehicle plunged from the woods. Ethan swung the car hard, and Tanner and Peter jarred against the door. The tires caught and put them out onto the road once more. Ethan didn't wait for everyone to recover but pressed the gas pedal to the floor as he gripped the wheel tighter. The engine screamed under the pressure of the added weight and Ethan's aggressive driving. He ignored it and wrenched it around the next bend, regaining control quickly as the rear fishtailed.

"Talk to me, Luke. Where are they?"

"Left down the dirt track. Fast."

Luke's heart slammed against his rib cage. He could hear the pain, though the cries grew quieter. His terror mounted—he was losing his pack and was stuck in a stupid metal box, unable to help them. Ethan almost missed the turn and took the corner far too fast. Everyone braced as the car raised on two wheels before slamming back onto the ground.

The tires struggled to find a good grip on the loose dirt, and Luke snarled as some momentum was lost. Ethan down-shifted and tried to get more torque to push them on. The pack came into view. Luke opened the door and leapt out, rolling a few times before he jumped to his feet and joined the fray.

A group of hooded people bearing magic-imbued clubs circled them. The pack had split into two groups. Some tried to protect the injured members who lay eerily still on the ground, while others attempted to drive the attackers off. All had their teeth bared and hackles raised.

Luke didn't think. He leapt onto the back of the closest attacker, wrapped his legs around the man's waist, and punched him in the head until he slumped onto the ground. His knuckles were bloody, but he had only just begun. One-armed or not, the shifter would not sit by and watch as his pack was slaughtered.

The hooded figures were all well-muscled men. Luke's wolf surged forward. He would do whatever it took to keep his pack safe. A particularly burly man faced him. A malicious grin revealed a pair of gold teeth and shark-like eyes. Had Luke been thinking straight, he would have seen how dangerous the man was, but all he saw were the still forms of his pack-mates.

The shifter matched the hooded figure's grin with his predatory one, and he gestured for him to come at him. He was aware that his friends were behind him somewhere, but they were irrelevant. The hooded man saw a lean teenager with a wolf's glint in his eyes and assumed that Luke would be an easy target, especially with the way he held his right hand.

The figure rushed Luke, who sidestepped at the last second and kicked the man hard in the lower back. He stumbled forward and Luke, using this advantage, swept his leg around to drive the assailant's legs out from under him. The man landed hard, face-down in the dirt, but was faster than Luke had anticipated. He rolled over and was almost back on his feet when the shifter booted him in the jaw.

Luke's wolf instincts screamed at him to debilitate his attacker, to incapacitate his legs and kill him with a blow to the throat. The man caught Luke's ankle as his head whipped to the side from the strike to his jaw. The shifter snarled and held his balance as the man yanked hard, trying to pull him down. Luke took a risk, put his weight onto the held leg, and directed everything he had into a vicious kick to the enemy's temple.

He landed flat on his back, but his adversary was out cold and a steady pool of blood blossomed around his head. He might have killed the man. The thought vanished quickly when a sharp pain exploded in his ribs. He spun around and saw the pack alpha leap at a smaller man's neck. The wolf sank his teeth deep into the blond man's throat and tore it out, ensuring he would never lay another hand on a shifter.

Tanner and Ethan worked as a unified pair. Tanner charged in and swung a fist at a tattooed man's face while Ethan called his magic and threw small shocks of lightning at him. Their opponent shouted in pain as the electricity scorched large burns over his increasingly pained body. Tanner backed off and called his magic. He wasn't as confident in offensive magic as some of his friends. While he much preferred defensive, the wolves behind him weren't moving. They needed medical attention fast.

He felt his magic fill him and focused on Professor Powell's lessons. An image of a trio of throwing knives rose in his mind. This was life or death, he reminded himself. There was no time to wonder if he was doing the right thing. The weapons formed as the tattooed man gathered himself to tackle Ethan. He paused, his eyes wide, as the blades whirled and buried themselves in his thighs.

He couldn't kill him. Tanner didn't have it in him. He wanted to help people, and the man couldn't hurt any more wolves with knives buried in his thighs.

Aya was truly vicious when she chose to be. She had practiced for this moment with her dolls for years. She took a deep breath and pictured the man's club colliding with the white wolf's head. Pulling her wand, she maintained the image of the wolf whining before it collapsed and summoned every scrap of magic she had at her disposal.

The assailant was easily twice her size, perhaps even larger, and packed with muscle. She would never stand a chance in a physical fight. It was a good thing she didn't intend to get into one. Keeping her wand steady and her magic flowing, she focused on the man, allowing the screams and sound of breaking bones to fade away.

With a delicate flick of her wrist, she lifted the man and heaved him into the heavy trunk of a nearby oak. The tree shuddered and rained leaves down around them. The man's bones cracked and crunched before he dropped to the bare earth at the base of the tree. His eyes rolled back in his head, and blood trickled from his mouth. Aya didn't give herself a chance to think about what she had just done. Her priority was saving the pack.

Emma and Kathleen tried to use every piece of healing magic they had learned over the years. The others focused on driving the attackers off, which gave them the opportunity to help the fallen wolves. Kathleen calmed her mind and tried to remember what Professor Hudson had taught them.

"I need to form the image of the injuries in my mind and use my magic to knit them back together," she whispered to herself.

She placed her hand gently on the ribs of a pale gray wolf. She was barely breathing, and Kathleen knew she needed to act. *Now.* She summoned her magic and closed her eyes, seeking the injuries with her mind—severe internal bleeding and badly broken ribs. Kathleen pushed her doubt aside and pressed her magic gently into the shattered body. She wouldn't allow her to die.

It took everything she had. Slowly, the image in her mind shifted to look more as it should. The organs knitted together, and the blood receded. Sweat beaded on Kathleen's forehead, and her breathing became labored. The wolf's ribs moved more easily beneath her hand. She was doing it. Kathleen made one final push, and the shifter opened her eyes. She was still in a lot of pain, but she'd survive the night.

The time had finally come. The shadow was coming for him. Ira could feel it skulking through the darkness outside his office. He had no choice but to make a run for the kemana. If he could reach the crystal, one tiny thread remained. All he needed was that thread and everything would fall into place, he was sure of it.

Ira steeled himself and ignored the dull throb in his head and the way he couldn't quite catch his breath. He was dying. His magic had deserted him, and his life force was slowly drained by the haunting shadow. If he could make it to the kemana, he might have a chance.

Opening his cottage door, he launched himself into the darkness and ran into the woods with everything he had. His life depended on it.

Jason had crept away from the dance, intending to try to get into Professor Heineken's cottage. Time was running out, and he needed to stop him before he could complete his final experiment. He was in the shadows outside the professor's cottage when the front door was thrown open and the man sprinted into the darkness as though the hounds of hell were on his heels.

For a second, Jason was torn between entering or following him. He ignored the cottage and chased after the professor into the shadowy depths of the forest. They ran between the mature trees. He could hear the cries of agony from the pack in the distance. Branches whipped past him and clawed at his flesh. Jason pushed on, ignoring the shadowy figure that seemed to haunt the professor. He would not let him out of his sight. This would all end that night.

Alison watched in horror as Luke leapt out of the car. A

group of hooded men was attacking his pack and each carried a club imbued with dark magic. She jumped from the vehicle the moment Ethan had slowed it enough. Her friends all rushed to defend the pack, but Alison paused. She saw something familiar.

A dark, shadowy figure lurked in the trees. She had convinced Professor Powell to allow her into the professor's library to research the dark magic related to his friend. What she hadn't told him was that she was really studying the shadow that had come out of the pendant. That same darkness now turned its attention to her, and a chill ran through Alison. She knew the malicious power was the one she had brought into the world, and she had to be the one to remove it again.

Alison called her magic. The shadow fled into the woods, and she ran after it. Her friends would protect the pack but she had to return this entity to where it had come from. The soft earth gave beneath her feet, enough to slow her down. She pushed errant branches aside with her magic, preventing them from snagging her.

Two more sets of footsteps echoed through the woods as the dark shape dipped between the trees. She didn't know if the others were working with it or hunting it like she was. The creature seemed to have a plan in mind. It never faltered or wavered in its path. Labored breathing caught Alison's attention, and she saw two figures running nearby. Suddenly, the shadow dove into the hidden entrance to the kemana. Alison gasped. There were too many innocent lives down there. She had wanted to capture it in the woods where it would be safer.

She bolted down the stairs into the darkness. Alison

had never seen the kemana unlit before. She saw the dimmed magic of the crystals and the souls of the inhabitants huddled near shops and pressed against the walls. The usual technicolor displays of magic were gone. It seemed dead and far colder than it had any right to be. The shadow was a black hole that moved with swift intent, deeper into the kemana. She paused for a moment, looking for a trap. This felt a little too convenient. The two people who had run through the woods with her crashed down the stairs.

Alison was torn between watching her target and her need to identify the newcomers. The shadow stopped and turned slowly to face her. No, not her—the man behind her. Alison glanced back to see Professor Heineken. Confusion filled her, then she remembered his plans to steal the magic from the kemana crystal. In her vision, he almost didn't exist. His magic was so faded that she almost couldn't discern it, and his life force flickered and dulled as she watched.

The black apparition appeared at her side. It reached out with one hand, and Alison saw Professor Heineken's life force leave his body and enter the dark hole. She pulled her magic and tried to push her Drow side aside in favor of light magic. This was a creature of death and destruction, and there was a very real chance that her dark magic would only fuel it. Alison struggled to clear her mind and find lightness. Her desire to destroy the entity was overwhelming her human instincts and pulling on her Drow power.

Jason Parker stepped around the professor and whispered as he pointed his wand at the shadow. His face was a mask of calm confidence like this was merely a stroll in the park. They were both too slow. Alison gasped when the professor's spirit was pulled into a rift that led to the World in Between. She heard his terrified screams of agony. The breach closed behind him and silence reigned over the kemana once more.

This was not a fight for gentle spells. Jason whispered the dark magic curse that would rip the shadow's very essence apart. Alison summoned her magic and began binding the darkness with light magic that burned the edges of the being. It stumbled backward and released a keening scream. Still, it refused to succumb without a fight and lashed out with what could only be described as death magic. Jason formed a strong barrier of light around himself and Alison. That cost him his focus, and he had to begin the curse once more.

He had no idea what the shadow was, but Alison fought it with a passion and fire that Jason hoped he'd never have to face himself. The Drow's eyes blazed with fury and power that made the entity hesitate and step back in fear before it tried to push forward once more. Its death magic whipped around them, clawing at the barrier. Jason held it with all he had while desperately whispering his curses. This was not a fight they could afford to lose.

Jason released the curse, and it struck the shadow where its heart should have been. The darkness shifted form and moved to wrap its hand around Alison's face. Her expression took on the countenance of a warrior fueled by righteous anger. Jason couldn't help but admire her at that moment. He refocused on the task at hand and quickly chanted another curse designed to undo a being's magic and destroy their life force.

Alison fought hard. She was relentless as she threw fireball after fireball at the shadow, driving it back toward the darkened crystal. Her fight was for all the people the being had killed. She fought for the pack and the pain they had endured. Alison would not give in or walk away until it was over.

The fear of the kemana inhabitants fueled the creature, making it stronger and more difficult to kill. Each strike Alison and Jason managed only caused temporary damage. It healed itself, pulling on the increasing terror around it. Jason released another curse. A hole appeared in the center of the entity, and they both pushed forward, finally seeing some hope. Alison never thought she'd see the day when she was happy to fight alongside a dark wizard, but his curses were working.

An Ifrit emerged from the darkness and trapped the fell creature, his fire bringing much-needed light and warmth. The Ifrit stared into the black depths of the being, and slowly, a toothy grin formed on his angular face. The darkness flickered and almost seemed to shudder as it looked back at its captor. Alison and Jason used the distraction to launch a combined attack. Her fireballs seared through its essence, and Jason's curses disintegrated the last threads of magic holding it together.

The shadow pulsed weakly and thinned into nothing more than a faint smoke. The lights flickered and slowly returned to the kemana. The crystal at the center began to glow softly and grew brighter with each passing moment. Life returned to the space around them. Alison watched as the bright ribbons of colorful magic flowed across the ceiling and along the walls. The kemana transformed before her eyes.

"Thank you." The Ifrit gave her a small nod before he vanished back between the stalls.

A cheer spread until it was almost a deafening roar. Alison grinned, and Jason maintained a small polite smile.

He stuffed his hands into his pockets. "We're not such a bad team. Although I would rather we didn't do this again."

Alison laughed, the sound harsh.

"You are the last person I expected to ally with."

Jason shrugged.

"Things change. I am freeing myself from my family. I'll travel the world and find my place within it. I don't regret learning the dark magic, but it's not the path I intend to follow. Not anymore. You and your friends showed me there's a better way." He looked away. "I'm sorry for what I did. There are no excuses, not really. I plan to devote my life to rectifying the damage I did and helping people. I'm not sure on the details yet, but I'll figure it out."

Alison couldn't believe what she was hearing. She had an odd understanding that in his own way, Jason now mirrored her path. She had turned from her Drow heritage to make the world a better place.

"I'm happy for you."

And she truly was. She couldn't imagine that being trapped in the cage his family had created would have given him a happy life. At least now, he was free.

CHAPTER TWENTY-SIX

Alison returned and found the hooded figures were all unconscious. A few of the pack members had been badly injured, but Kathleen had pulled them back from the brink. The headmistress and a few other professors, including the shifter, Professor Hodges, had heard the chaos and come to help.

The headmistress looked at Alison. "Why am I not surprised to find you here, Miss Brownstone? You seem to be found around trouble a lot."

"Luke's pack was attacked. We couldn't sit by and let them be hurt." Alison folded her arms. "We heard them and came to help."

"You stole the car. Again." Professor Powell looked at Ethan. "We need a better lock on the workshop."

"And if we hadn't stolen the car and made it here, who knows what would have happened to my pack." Luke stared Professor Powell down. "We look after our own. Pack bonds are tighter than any blood bond."

"You do understand that lives were lost here tonight?"

Professor Powell's look challenged the students. "Questions will be asked about these hooded attackers."

"We were defending the pack. Any court would understand that." Alison went to Luke. "We stand by our actions."

"Does she speak for all of you?" Professor Powell looked at Kathleen. "Will you all stand in court and defend the fact that you took two lives tonight?"

The headmistress glared at Xander. "That's enough. You've made your point."

"Since we saved the day, does this mean we get an extra special breakfast tomorrow?" Ethan grinned.

"No, it does not. Head back to the school and go to bed."

They had been hailed as heroes throughout the school. Alison had hidden for most of it. No one asked where Professor Heineken had gone. The headmistress had given Alison a knowing look, and she was sure that Ms. Berens would have a private chat with her in the not too distant future. She hadn't seen Jason around either. He must have been in the school somewhere, but he had a way of hiding when he chose to do so.

Alison didn't like the attention. She already felt uncomfortable with the younger students' whispers about her role in the fight against the dark wizards the previous year. The pack had been grateful but not too showy, which she appreciated. Professor Hudson had tried to convince Kathleen to change her focus from fashion to healing given her extraordinary gift. She had rolled her eyes at the thought. There was little to no glory in healing after all.

The day had passed slowly, and Alison was grateful when the night descended. Peace settled over the school, and the stars came out, making her smile. They gave her a connection to Izzie, something she really needed after this last ordeal. Her friend would have understood how exhausting it was to maintain the polite smile through the story again and again. Alison was far happier saving the day from the shadows.

Everyone was fast asleep, and she slipped her shoes on for one last midnight stroll. She wanted to say goodbye to Horace and Dorvu and took time to gaze at the familiar, gently rolling grounds around the large school. The mountains on the horizon seemed a little farther away that night. Alison allowed the feeling of peace to descend. This was her walking meditation, her stolen moments of quiet and calm. The dragon wheeled about overhead and put on an acrobatic display that brought a smile to her face. She would miss him far more than she was willing to admit.

Horace patted the bench beside him and gave Alison a gentle smile. His scruffy dog lay at his feet, and a small fire crackled not too far away. Thankfully, the only dead animals recently had belonged to Dorvu.

"This is the last of our little chats, isn't it?" Horace looked into the fire. "You're ready to move onto the next stage of your life."

Dorvu landed and walked up to her. "Is it really the last one?"

Alison smiled warmly. "I'm afraid so. Don't worry. I'm sure you'll make new friends."

The dragon frowned. "None of them will be quite like you."

"And there will never be another one like you, Dorvu."

She put her hand on his snout. "But we'll always have our memories."

The dragon thought on that. Finally, he puffed out a small cloud of cold air and settled himself, apparently satisfied with the state of things.

They sat in silence for a short while before Alison felt she was ready. It was time to move on.

"Thank you, Horace. You have been a wonderful friend over the years. You helped me through some dark times, and I can't express how grateful I am for that. The students...we're all very lucky to have you."

He smiled and patted her knee.

"That's what I'm here for. You'll always be welcome to stop by and have a chat."

Alison thought that maybe she would take him up on that one day.

Luke rolled his shoulders and tried to ignore the twinge in his bad wrist. It was healing, and Kathleen had managed to help it some, but he still couldn't put any real weight on it. He looked at his teammates who were all bright-eyed and eager to enter the game. They had insisted he play this match as their captain. He took great pride in that role, and he was determined not to let them down.

"I feel like I'm supposed to give a grand speech here, but I'm not that good with words." Luke shrugged. "So, er, let's go kick ass!"

They jogged out onto the field to uproarious applause from the crowd. Some of the spectators had made signs to encourage the team. Luke appreciated the effort and support. A swell of pride rose within him. It had been a difficult year, and the last few months had been even more so. Now, it was his time to shine. Louper had been his chance to step out of the box that surrounded him and really push the boundaries.

The scene wrapped around them and Luke took a moment to figure out where on earth they were. Dark-blue water glittered beneath a bright sun. The ground rocked, and a strong breeze cut across the open space around them. He looked at the wood planking beneath his feet and realized they were on a boat. He'd never stepped foot on one before, and the movement of the sea took some adjustment. Wolves were land animals, and this felt very wrong.

Cody grinned and pointed at the jolly roger flag above them. "We're on a pirate ship. That is so freakin' cool."

"All right, you know the drill. A ship means the rival team can't be too far away. This is the championship, and we're in this to win it. Etienne, get us a tracking spell. Cody and Daniel, summon up some defenses. There are likely to be pirates around here. Matt, check for any scents that might be useful."

The team got to work immediately and made Luke proud. Cody and Daniel's magic and confidence had grown by leaps and bounds. Their fireballs hovered, ready for any attacker. Etienne's distinctive purple tracking arrow popped up and vibrated as it pointed toward the cabin on their left. Booted footsteps crashed toward them, and Luke gestured for them to remain quiet and enter the cabin.

Cody swung the wooden hatch open and sent a pair of

fireballs ahead to clear any enemies. The team descended the creaky stairs and found themselves in a low-ceilinged room that Luke was sure rocked far more than the top deck did.

The arrow guided them through a space packed with foul-smelling barrels that oozed something deep-green. The boots now chased them and grew steadily closer. Luke didn't want to fight if he didn't have to, not one-armed.

"Barricade the door." He pointed at a barrel. "Matt, here."

The shifter lifted the barrel and planted it in front of the entrance before they followed the arrow once more. The door rattled as fists pounded on it, and deep growling voices shouted in a language Luke couldn't understand.

They followed the guide deeper into the belly of the ship. The lights dimmed and the swaying increased, affecting their balance.

"Wait." Matt held up a hand. "Listen."

Luke pricked his ears and heard it—the soft clicking of something moving toward them. Scratching noises skittered along the walls. The lights went out, leaving them with the glow of the arrow and the wizards' fireballs.

Skeletons unfolded themselves from the edges of the room and appeared from behind hammocks.

"Oh, come on, really?" Cody threw his first fireball at one.

Etienne summoned a pair of swords and handed one to Luke.

"You're not completely useless yet, captain." The elf smirked. "Make us proud."

Luke bit back a sarcastic comment and laughed. The elf had attitude but he meant well.

Matt fought with a ferocity only a shifter possessed. He tore the skeletons apart with his bare hands while Luke swung his sword left-handed. He cut through some of the attackers, but he could admit that it really came down to his team.

They fought their way through and into the final treasure room. That was when they saw their opponents for the first time. The New Orleans Cougars barreled into the room from the far door. The purple arrow vanished, having done its job. The gold token was somewhere in that room. The only problem was that the room was full of gold —coins, goblets, jewelry, chests, and every other shape and form you could possibly imagine. The metal reflected the light back from the wizards' fireballs.

Both teams looked around and tried to assess their chances. Luke and Matt sniffed the air, and the captain's instincts kicked in. He rushed across the room to the west corner where he pushed his way past a heavy chest and ducked to find a small crawlspace. He wriggled through and emerged in a small, dark room. Once his eyes adjusted, he saw he was in a closet. The walls were covered with clothes he ignored. They weren't hiding the token.

Luke crept forward and opened the door to peer into what appeared to be the captain's quarters. A large desk made of dark wood and polished to a bright shine stood beneath a window that stretched the length of the far wall. Maps curled on the tabletop in the center of the room, but it was the simple wooden pedestal that caught his attention

—a plain pillar with a square tabletop. It seemed to stand out amidst the far grander furniture around it.

Someone was coming. He heard heavy footsteps approach the entrance. There was no more time to investigate for traps. The air temperature shifted behind him— someone approached from behind him, too. Luke darted into the room and saw a large pirate, complete with a black hat and wooden peg leg, enter from the passageway. The man saw him and moved with far more speed than someone with a wooden limb had any right to. He rushed at Luke with his hand extended and holding a sword. The shifter rolled over the table and ducked beneath the vicious swing before he lunged forward and grabbed the golden token.

He held it high above him and grinned unabashedly at the crowds. Everyone was on their feet, screaming their congratulations and applauding for him and the team. Cody and the others ran over to Luke and lifted him onto their shoulders. He'd done it. He had taken his team to the championship and won.

Coach Regency strode across the field with a big trophy in his hands. He offered it to Luke who lifted it with his one hand.

The shifter grinned at his teammates. "I couldn't have done it without you. You've done the school and me proud."

They lowered him to the ground, and Etienne hugged him, whispering, "I said you weren't useless."

Luke laughed and punched the elf jokingly in the arm. He couldn't believe it. They'd pulled it off.

CHAPTER TWENTY-SEVEN

A lison took her time descending the stairs into the kemana. She admired the beautiful rainbow array of magic. The crystal had been completely restored, and the underground city was vibrant and full of life once more. It was as though nothing had happened. Alison paused at the bottom of the stairs as the memory of Professor Heineken's screams echoed in her mind.

Tanner put his arm around her waist and offered her quiet comfort. She had told him everything. After the shadow from the pendant, she hadn't wanted to hide anything.

"Are you okay?" He held her away from the main crowd, providing a safe space. "Do you want to leave?"

"No, I'm okay." She exhaled slowly. "It threw me for a moment, that's all. This is our last chance to be here together, and I want to enjoy it."

Kathleen grinned, pulled her wand out, and pointed it at her dress.

"We're completely free to use our magic. Which means we can have some fun."

She focused, and her dress turned from a demure slate gray affair down to her knees into a fluttery pale-blue affair that barely reached halfway down her thigh. She grinned and looked exceptionally pleased with herself.

Emma shook her head and turned her attention to the stalls and shops around them.

"Where shall we head first?"

"Why don't we wander? We're not in a rush after all," Tanner answered, squeezing Alison gently.

They headed down the less-traveled right street and took their time admiring the wares. Ethan quickly grew bored with browsing and formed orbs of light which he bounced around, doing acrobatic tricks in the air—until two of them struck a wood elf in the back of the head. The elf glared at Ethan, who smiled innocently. The wounded party didn't buy it for a second but let it slide.

Aya used her magic to pick up a striking white wand with an intricate blood-red inlay. "Now you're showing off." Alison smiled at her. "I don't think it's your style, though. What about the pretty oak one?"

Aya returned the wand and inspected a plainer oak version with a rose carved into the handle. She weighed it in her hand and frowned.

"No, it's not the right one."

They continued through the kemana, pausing at their favorite crepe place before they continued. Alison summoned her magic after Kathleen and Peter nagged her to do so. She began by forming a gag around Kathleen's mouth, amusing everyone. Kathleen glared but said nothing, much to the group's relief. They didn't want a fight, not that day.

Black ribbons slithered into existence and danced around Alison's arms, settling between her shoulder blades where they shifted into delicate black wings. She grew more comfortable with her magic. It was something she needed to refine, as Professor Powell had demonstrated, but she was improving.

Kathleen dragged everyone into a high-end jewelry store which Alison refused to step foot in. She leaned against the wall, people-watching, when she noticed a shady-looking man around the same age as Professor Powell with scruffy grey stubble along his jaw and deep-set, dark eyes.

Alison followed him down a darker, narrow alley between two sections of the kemana. The stalls there were already closed for the day. Shadows filled the corners and claimed the edges, hiding who knew what. Alison remained focused on the man whom she was sure was the dark wizard Professor Powell had talked about. He had hurt Luke and killed many people over the years.

Her magic came quickly and easily. Alison intended to bind him so that she could interrogate him. She formed ropes and began wrapping them around his upper body. An invisible wave of magic struck her and threw her back against the wall, the air exploding from her lungs. Alison coughed and drew on the anger that filled her, strengthening her magic. Her desire for destruction added depth and power to her magic.

The man turned to face her. His eyes shone when he saw her magic. Alison saw his were utterly pitch-black, without a shred of light. She'd never seen someone work with pure dark magic before. His soul was equally as black, incapable of compassion or any form of caring.

Alison created a pair of daggers and closed on the man. He stepped toward her and began moving his hands. She saw his magic this time. It weaved into a tight spiral before it unfurled quickly and a set of throwing knives hurtled toward her head. Alison stood strong and formed a shield, then pitched her daggers at him. She wouldn't roll over and allow this man to walk away.

Tanner seemed to come out of nowhere.

"Alison?"

That was all it took. The man formed his magic before Alison could wrap Tanner in a shield. He was thrown against the wall and enveloped in the wizard's darkness. Alison ran to him, her heart pounding in her chest. Tanner's eyes were open but unseeing. His pulse was weak and his breathing shallow.

Her adversary launched another curse at her. She felt the enchantment slip beneath her skin, but her magic protected her. Fury coursed through her veins. She straightened and wrapped the full extent of her power around her like a vengeful goddess. The wizard's eyes widened. Alison launched everything she had at him with the intention to destroy him from the inside out.

He formed a shield and continued to cast smaller curses at her as he backed out the alley. Alison went to follow him and hunt him down, but Tanner lay too still. She ran to him and put her hand on his chest. Alison tried to break the magic that encircled him, but it wouldn't budge. She couldn't feel Tanner beneath it. His soul was consumed and buried by the darkness.

"Tanner? Please, Tanner, you have to wake up."

Alison swallowed hard and shook him.

"You have to wake up!"

"Alison?" Peter stood beside her.

"A dark wizard attacked us. He's bound Tanner in something. I can't make him wake up."

"We need to get him to the infirmary." Peter crouched down. "Alison, did you hear me?"

"Yes. Help me."

Peter put his arm under Tanner and together, they carried him out of the alley. Alison was tempted to track and destroy the wizard who had done this to him. She saw the concern on her friends' faces, though, and knew she had to stay with Tanner. The wizard would return. He was there for Professor Powell and wouldn't go far.

Alison refused to leave Tanner's side. He lay too still on the plain white bed and his skin looked frighteningly pale. The nurse tried to send her away, but she wouldn't budge. The headmistress and Professor Powell came into the infirmary with grave expressions on their faces.

"How is he? I have been told he was subject to a dark wizard's attack." Mara spoke quietly to the nurse.

"I'm afraid he's in a magically induced coma. I have no idea how to do anything more than make him comfortable. Miss Brownstone has tried to break the spell to no avail."

Mara looked at Alison with deep sympathy. The girl sat holding Tanner's hand with a look of grim determination on her face. Unshed tears glistened in the corners of her eyes.

"Alison, what happened?" Mara spoke clearly, trying to snap the student out of her daze.

Alison drew a deep breath and described the incident with the dark wizard.

"I saw his dark magic and wanted to stop him. The kemana had already been under attack once. Tanner came into the alley, and I couldn't react quickly enough. The dark magic encircled him like a spider's silk around a fly caught in its web."

Mara felt that was all too accurate. She couldn't see the dark magic the way Alison could, but she could feel Tanner and how deeply buried his weak life force was. Mara had never seen anything like it before, and it concerned her that the nurse was at a loss. Xander was uncomfortably silent.

The headmistress took his arm and led him to a quiet corner where she boxed him in and glared at him until he broke.

"I'm sorry, Mara, but I think I know the wizard who Alison encountered. I fear that it was my fault that she followed him in the first place." Xander leaned back against the wall. "Do you remember Robert?"

Mara narrowed her eyes. "The weaselly man whom you, James, and the others used to spend far too much time with?"

"Yes. He was part of our small group. We practiced dark magic together. I suspected that he was the wrong personality, but I was young and foolish and enjoyed the power trip that came with using him as an errand boy. Things went horribly wrong. He killed Lynn, and so we stripped him of his magic—or so we thought."

Xander lowered his eyes.

"Do you remember when we were attacked while we were camping?"

"Yes."

"That was Robert. We...I don't know how he did it, but somehow, he managed to fill his magic reserves with pure dark magic. It's unlike anything I've seen before. He has systematically killed our group over the last decade. He came here to kill us. I've been hunting him, but he keeps evading me."

"And exactly how is Alison involved in this?"

"She saw me weaving a dark magic spell to try and trap him. I told her the story so that she would understand that I wasn't using again, not really."

"You brought a student into the hunt for a very dangerous dark wizard so she wouldn't think badly of you?" Mara poked him in the chest. "Have I got that right?"

She was seething. Xander could be reckless and arrogant at times, but this was something else. Not only had he put her life at risk, but he had also endangered a student, and now, a young man was in a magical coma.

"I'm sorry. I was trying to protect you." Xander reached for Mara's face.

She slapped his hand away.

"I do not need your protection, Xander Powell. You know that. I am more than capable of looking after myself, you arrogant fool."

Creases formed between his brows. Mara sighed and calmed herself.

"That was inappropriate. You should have told me. This is my school. The students are under my protection. You owed me that information." She saw the tension growing in Xander's jaw. "Don't you dare try and compare this to my hiding Izzie's bloodline from you."

They both sighed, and Mara stepped back, giving Xander room.

"That boy might never wake up," she said softly.

CHAPTER TWENTY-EIGHT

A lison stood at her window, lost in thought. Tanner might never wake up. A gap year before college seemed like a thoroughly reckless idea now. She wanted to go to college, learn all she could and seek out who did this to her first love. Search for an antidote, but Brownstone had already told her that sometimes these things take time, and she had to go on with her life. Shay had chimed in on the phone with the idea that more knowledge made her even more powerful. See it as another tool in her arsenal, but that her father was right. It was also going to take some courage to go on with her life, and even let happiness be a part of it.

Like her graduation day.

She couldn't believe the day had really arrived. The girls had put on pretty dresses and comfortable shoes before they draped their graduation robes over the top. Alison knew Shay and Brownstone were outside waiting for her. They'd flown in from L.A. to watch the ceremony, eager to see her. She couldn't believe her journey at the school was coming to an end.

The guys waited for them at the top of the stairs. Alison looked automatically for Tanner, and her chest constricted when he wasn't there. He was still in the infirmary, locked in a magical coma. He was being moved to a hospital that night. Alison had stopped by to say goodbye to him the night before. He'd had such a bright future ahead of him, and they'd planned to remain close at Georgetown. That was all taken away in the blink of an eye.

Kathleen put her arm around Alison's shoulder and gave her a sad smile.

"Don't cry. You need to look beautiful for your graduation." She stroked her hair out of her eyes. "Your parents are here, right?"

Alison nodded.

"Yeah, Shay and James flew in." She choked down the tears and focused on the graduation. Tanner wouldn't want her to be upset.

They made their way down the stairs, and Ethan proudly showed Alison a sign he'd painted that said, I don't even go here. Alison laughed, more for his sake than with genuine humor. Peter had opted for, "I is smart" on his, whereas Aya chose, "I still have no idea what I'm doing."

Alison composed herself. This was a huge moment in her life. She had a big future ahead of her after all.

The students made their way into the auditorium and took their places in their assigned seats. The headmistress stepped onto the stage wearing a beautiful navy-blue dress and with her hair fashioned into a pretty up-do. Alison hadn't seen her put in quite so much effort before.

"Today, we are here to celebrate the ascension of these fine students to the next stage of their life. They have each made us proud, and we are honored to have been a part of their lives. We're sure they will all play a key role in shaping the world around us to be a brighter and better place." The headmistress waited for the applause to stop before she began calling the students' names.

Ethan wasn't one to miss an opportunity for a prank. He had been more careful this time, especially after the April Fool's joke. After extensive study, he'd decided on something that would be memorable without causing too much chaos.

He ran this thumb over his focus bands as he whispered the spell beneath his breath. He'd laid the groundwork after everyone had gone to bed the night before. To the headmistresses' dismay, the diplomas sprouted wings and flew around the room. Each had a unique set of wings, ranging from pure-white dove wings to brightly colored parrot wings. Ethan had worked hard to make each reflect the student to whom the diploma belonged. He was an artist in his own way.

The headmistress glared at him. "Ethan, I assume this is your doing. It's not too late for me to hold you back."

Ethan's jaw dropped. She couldn't, could she?

"I happen to think it shows remarkable magical talent and creativity," a female voice said. "I would be interested in speaking to this Ethan."

He swallowed hard. The headmistress narrowed her eyes before she snapped her fingers, and Ethan's spell was broken. The diplomas returned to where they belonged.

"That is between you and Ethan," she replied before she called up the first student.

When Alison was called, she walked onto the stage with a bright smile that didn't quite reach her eyes. She accepted her diploma and turned to look for Shay and James. Her mother gave her a small wave, and the weight on her shoulders eased a little. Her friends had been good to her and had fought at her side, but there were some things only your parents understood or could help with.

Kathleen attempted to give a small acceptance speech, but the headmistress ushered her off the stage, reminding her this wasn't an awards ceremony. Once everyone had received their diploma and the students were free to wander, Alison found her adopted parents. Brownstone was easy to spot. His intimidating appearance meant that people allowed him a lot of room.

Shay hugged Alison tightly and stroked her hair as the emotions welled up again. Alison knew that graduation would be difficult without Tanner, but it constantly took her by surprise. They guided her over to a quiet corner where she returned to her usual fierce self. She pulled on her anger and allowed it to overwhelm the sadness and bitterness threatening to consume her.

"The dark wizard who attacked Tanner goes by the name of Robert, and he's a former associate of Xander Powell. Not a lot to go on, I know. His magic is pure dark magic, and he's been corrupted by it. I know what you said on the phone, but I can't wait till I get through college. I need you to promise me you'll hunt him down and bring him to justice." Alison held Brownstone's gaze, refusing to look away.

Brownstone smiled, admiring the ferocity of his adopted daughter. She had never been a meek little girl or a spoiled princess. She had always had a fire within her that many combat witches would envy. He looked at her at that moment and understood that if he didn't hunt the wizard down, she would. Alison would devote every living moment to finding him and ending him. He couldn't let her throw her life away like that, not with the bright future she had ahead of her.

"I promise. I will use every resource at my disposal to ensure he is brought to justice."

She smiled and breathed again.

"Now..." Shay pulled a shiny bag from behind her back. "We have more pleasant things to deal with. We have some graduation gifts for you and a little something to remember the musical. We have to thank Mara for sending us a video of it. Your father has watched it over a dozen times."

Brownstone smiled at his daughter.

Alison took the bag from Shay and sat, giving them her full attention.

"Your father spent a long time deliberating over these, so I hope you like them."

"I'm sure I'll love them." She smiled and opened the envelope first.

It took her a long moment to understand exactly what she was looking at. The numbers were ridiculously large and didn't mean much of anything until she realized it was a bank statement. Her bank statement.

"I moved the money from your mother and father, and then I doubled it to make sure that you never need to get into foolish situations because of funds. You'll have the freedom you deserve." Brownstone smiled. "That is your money to do whatever you want."

Alison wouldn't need to work for decades if she didn't want to. She still would, of course. She couldn't imagine not working, but knowing that she didn't need to worry was something of a relief.

The next box was long and slender. Alison had a reasonable idea what it was but didn't say anything. She unwrapped the silky black paper and opened the brown leather box to reveal a stunning dagger.

"That is an old Drow artifact." Shay picked it up out of the box. "There are only three in existence. It'll work with your magic to hone it and search out your enemy's weaknesses. In a fight, you will be unstoppable."

Alison ran her fingertips over the blood-red hilt and took it from her mother, feeling the weight of it in her hand. It was beautifully balanced and the perfect size for her.

"It's stunning, thank you."

Shay handed her a small, square box next. Alison opened it to reveal a silver necklace with a circular, blue stone pendant. Alison saw the magic locked within the crystal. She marveled at how much magic they had managed to squeeze into it and noticed the protective web and matrix of a complicated shield.

"This will stop anyone from being able to touch or steal your magic." Brownstone lifted it from the box.

Alison tilted her head forward and held her hair out of the way, allowing her father to place the necklace around her neck. She felt the warm thrum of the magic and immediately felt more secure.

Shay handed her the final two boxes. Alison opened the first and found a charm of a witch's hat. "Never forget that appearances can be deceiving," said Shay. "The lesson from Wicked."

Alison smiled and opened the second box. Inside were a pair of intricately made wing earrings—one black and one pure white. She saw the delicate strands of fairy magic threaded between each hand-made feather on the wings. Her breath was immediately stolen by the sheer detail they had added into such small pieces of art.

"They're incredible, thank you."

"Your father wanted to give you something beautiful, as a woman. You're a fighter, but you're so much more. He wanted to make sure you knew that."

Alison set the earrings down carefully and put her arms around her father's neck, hugging him tightly.

"Thank you, for everything."

Brownstone held her gently, feeling a great deal of love for both his daughter and his wife at that moment.

"Hi, the memorial is starting in a minute," Aya said quietly.

Shay put Alison's gifts away safely, and they followed Aya out onto the grounds where the memorial was just beginning. It was a somber affair held in memory of Lisa, the student who lost her life during the fight against the dark wizards the previous year. The headmistress unveiled a plaque honoring the girl's memory. They watched as a building was renamed after her and gentle applause spread through the crowd. Her life was lost, but she would not be forgotten.

After the memorial, a big party blossomed in the beautiful warm sunshine on the school grounds. Peter's butterflies provided the music, and the kitchen pixies had arranged a feast. Students and parents mingled, laughing and sharing stories of their adventures in the school. Alison remained a little distant from it all, watching without participating.

A feeling of closeness with Izzie formed, seemingly from nowhere. The headmistress skirted the crowd and ushered Alison quietly inside. Alison frowned and tried to push aside the spark of hope that maybe Izzie had returned. She missed her best friend and wanted desperately to see her again.

Alison stepped into the library and saw not only Izzie but what looked like her entire family. Professor Powell was there, along with Izzie's mother and Yumfuck, the little troll who was now cursing up a storm.

Izzie raced across the room and threw her arms around her, pulling her into a fierce hug that squashed the air from both girls' lungs. They held each other tightly for a few minutes, not daring let go for fear of losing each other again.

"Oh, Alison, it's so good to see you. You wouldn't believe the adventures I've had, and I hear you've had some yourself."

"It's been a crazy year. Dark wizards, rogue shifters... you wouldn't believe it if I told you."

Izzie laughed and took Alison by the hand.

"I've worked on my diploma while we've been traveling and I'm here for my graduation. I don't get a fancy robe like you, but I had to see you."

Luke and the others burst into the library. Izzie left Alison's side to run to Luke, who kept his injured wrist carefully out of the way. They buried their faces in each other's necks and whispered things Alison was sure she didn't want to hear. Izzie's family were all present, as far as she could tell, although she wasn't entirely sure who some of them were.

Izzie's mother, Leira Berens, greeted her with a crooked smile. "Alison, it's so good to see you. We can't stay long, though. The forces that are hunting us will find us if we stay too long. Izzie wanted to be here to see you on your big day, and it was too important for her to miss. Can't stop living, ever."

Luke and Izzie had finally released each other, and everyone watched as the headmistress handed Izzie her diploma. A round of cheers sounded, and the girl found herself enveloped in a group hug.

Izzie laughed. "I wish we could stay a little longer." She hugged her friend one last time before she kissed Luke.

Alison watched as she headed off to who knew where through another portal with her family around her. Happiness thrummed through her knowing that Izzie was well and surrounded by good people. It wasn't the way she would have chosen for things to happen, but she remained happy nonetheless.

The moment that everyone had dreaded finally arrived. They gathered on the circular driveway with their bags piled around them. It was time to say goodbye.

Kathleen hugged Alison tightly and wiped her eyes furiously.

"This isn't goodbye, okay? I know what I said about being too busy in New York, but we'll make time for each other. You hear?"

"We'll meet up regularly. You'll have to show me around the kemana there."

"Yes, and I'll make sure you are the best-dressed bounty hunter."

Alison laughed, imagining fighting dark wizards in frilly blouses and ridiculous boots.

Kathleen hugged her one last time moved on to say goodbye to Emma.

Luke sighed heavily. He still wasn't quite sure what he would do with his life. Everyone around him would go to college, but he would spend the summer at home to heal. He'd put off starting college for a year to give himself a chance to figure everything out and get his head straight. Seeing Izzie had made him think that maybe traveling to see the world would be good for him.

Peter and Kathleen went back and forth about who everyone should go to for tours of New York City. They would both be based there, and both were adamant they'd be the better tour guide.

"Of course I'd be the better guide. I know all the good places. I run in the right circles," Kathleen insisted, folding her arms.

"She'll take you to all the boring places with uptight

people and expensive cocktails." Peter spread his arms wide. "I'll take you to the fun places that show you the real New York."

"The real New York will get you stabbed." Kathleen sniffed.

"We have magic." Peter shrugged.

Alison would miss the banter between her friends. She saw Dorvu overhead, watching them. He landed nearby and grinned.

"I'll miss you all. No one could be better friends than you." The dragon tucked his wings in. "But I will be nice to the other students."

Aya placed her hand gently on his head. "We'll miss you too, Dorvu. Maybe we can visit sometime."

When all the goodbyes had been said and emotions ran high, Alison packed her bags into her parents' car and cast one last look at the large manor that had been her school and a kind of home. It was time to begin the next stage of her life and become a kickass bounty hunter. She would find who hurt Tanner and fulfill her own dreams, no matter how long it took. She was ready to embrace her future and shape the world into a better place.

The End

Alison's days at the School are over, but that's not the end of her story. Nor the end of adventures at the School.

*Stay tuned for TWO new series heading your way.
Alison is all grown-up and ready to take on the world.*

And the School of Necessary Magic gets some fresh blood with a new class of Freshmen.

Until then, have you had a chance to read the adventures of Shay, Alison's mentor and wife of Brownstone? If not, you can get book 1: <u>Kill the Willing</u> on Amazon.

Alison has graduated and is off to explore the world, go to college, see where she fits in among the general population of the new world order. Wondering what happens next? Well, we got you covered. Starting **December 4th** is the new series, **Alison Brownstone**, fresh out of college, opening her own bounty hunter business but with a twist on the old man's game. (You remember him. That dude, James Brownstone) She'll be a chip off the old block with a few Drow tricks in her bag to use as well. That's right, we have loads more stories to tell.

In the meantime, by the time this comes out I hope I got to see a lot of your faces in Las Vegas at the 20Books Author event. It's shaping up to be a nice gathering of some good folks (and a bunch of crazy authors).

I'll be back at work, typing as fast as I can with plans to get on my green bike now that I've gotten it back from the Offspring. He needed it for a prop in a Jackie Venson music video. We're a very artsy family, doing our own thing. I used to be able to ride a bike, leaning over as far as it could go, sure of myself and hands barely touching the bike.

But, ever since I had a lot of the muscle removed from the left leg after cancer, I have psyched myself out and do the widest right and left turns possible, a little too afraid of stopping the bike. Still, to my credit I keep trying, sure I'll get back the magic. First time I got back on a bike I kept falling over, hitting the pavement. Yes, I kept getting right back on because I knew if I didn't, I never would and that's not how I roll.

Finally, someone said, try getting off on the other side – the side with the whole leg. Voila! So much to unpack in that little story. Something about not giving up, courage to just go do it no matter how I look, and missing the obvious about trying the easier path, or in this case, easier side of the bike. Those are the kind of things I want to put into the stories I tell because in the end, the greatest asset we all have is the welcoming cooperation we can offer each other. Don't see how that's related?

It's because of all of you, part of my tribe in this world that I approach life with an open and optimistic curiosity. A belief that all is well so let's grow bigger and just trust that all is well. Without that as a baseline, too much time is spent wondering what could go wrong, instead of wondering what will go right. Vital difference to a life that continues to expand.

It's all possible because I surround myself with people who have the same kind of wonder and trust in the possibilities life has to offer. Just get up and get out there, see what's being offered.

That's why I keep getting back on that green Schwinn. I just know, it's gonna be a great ride in the end. More adventures to follow.

OTHER SERIES IN THE ORICERAN
UNIVERSE:

SCHOOL OF NECESSARY MAGIC
THE DANIEL CODEX SERIES
I FEAR NO EVIL
THE UNBELIEVABLE MR. BROWNSTONE
THE LEIRA CHRONICLES
REWRITING JUSTICE
THE KACY CHRONICLES
MIDWEST MAGIC CHRONICLES
SOUL STONE MAGE
THE FAIRHAVEN CHRONICLES

BOOKS BY MICHAEL ANDERLE

For a complete list of books by Michael Anderle, please visit

www.lmbpn.com/ma-books/

All LMBPN Audiobooks are Available at Audible.com and iTunes. For a complete list of audiobooks visit:

www.lmbpn.com/audible

www.ingramcontent.com/pod-product-compliance
Lightning Source LLC
Chambersburg PA
CBHW050240110726
47898CB00007B/2224